The Aristobrats

Jennifer Solow

sourcebooks
jabberwocky

Published by Sourcebooks Jabberwocky, an imprint of Sourcebooks, Inc.
P.O. Box 4410, Naperville, Illinois 60567-4410
(630) 961-3900
Fax: (630) 961-2168
www.jabberwockykids.com

Library of Congress Cataloging-in-Publication data is on file with the publisher.

Source of Production: Versa Press, East Peoria, Illinois, USA
Date of Production: August 2010
Run Number: 13086

Printed and bound in the United States of America.
VP 10 9 8 7 6 5 4 3 2 1

For Tommy, Griffin, and Tallulah

.

Part

Semper Veritas

Chapter 1

"Exsqueeze-ay moi? Some people are getting dressed in here…"

Parker Bell's mother, Ellen, had an unfortunate habit of opening her daughter's door without knocking. Parker was still in her pajamas and her room was a mess. Clothing rejects were all over the floor, draped over the antique chaise and dangling from the mahogany Darcy chair. The desk looked like something had exploded on it, and maybe it had—Parker seriously couldn't remember.

Ellen, a neat freak who'd have a hairy nip fit if the Egyptian cotton bath towels weren't folded in thirds, frowned at the unrecognizable floor and the searing beauty tools on the furniture. She looked like she might crack in half.

"I may need a search party the next time I come in here, Park."

Parker offered a morsel of wisdom she'd read once in *CosmoGirl*. "They say a messy room is the sign of a brilliant mind, Mom." She tossed a feather-light pashmina into the air and watched it float gracefully onto the ground.

Ellen ignored her compulsion to pick up and fold. "Then you must be a very smart girl," she said.

"Thank you." Parker grinned. Another mother-daughter point: scored.

"I just came in to tell you," Ellen said calmly, "that Armada will be driving you to school tomorrow because I have a meeting at Siddie's in the morning."

Siddie was Sir Sidmund Stryker, aka Sid Stryker, the front man of the legendary band, the Rebels. And Ellen was his architect. Sid hadn't made a public appearance in nearly a decade, ever since his mother published her tell-all memoir, *Rebel Without a Cause: My Life with Sid Stryker*. He'd begun renovating the old mansion he bought in Wallingford around the same time and now it was nearly finished. There were only a few people in the world the rock star trusted and Ellen was one of them. She had the alarm code to his house, the floor plans for his bedroom, swatches of fabric for his curtains, and her own schnuggly name for him. Parker found it all a little embarrassing.

"Why tomorrow?" Parker asked. She shouldn't have cared either way; it wasn't like she *needed* her mother to drive her to school. It was the first day of eighth grade, not kindergarten.

"I can move my meeting, sweetheart..." Ellen softened her tone. "If you want me to?" She seemed almost hopeful.

"You don't need to move your meeting." Parker tried to sound convincing. Sid was her mother's only client—Parker knew she had to make accommodations. "It's just school, Mom. No biggie."

She collapsed onto her bed and kicked off the furry slippers, looking up through the sheer drapery panels of her canopy bed toward the cottage chandelier that hung from the middle of the ceiling. The polished crystals sparkled in the morning sun. She tried to channel her inner-hypnotist: *I am Parker Bell. I am confident, cool, and on top of things.*

Ellen cleared a space for herself on the corner of the bed

next to Parker's school uniform. The black watch plaid kilt was made from fine merino wool instead of the cheap polyblend you get now, and the knife pleats were sharper and narrower than the newer ones. It was completely impossible to come by the pure wool version of the Wallingford Academy uniform, unless of course it had been handed down to you.

Parker was a third-generation Wally—one of just a handful of legacy students at the school: an Aristobrat, as most non-legacies called them, usually behind their backs. The title had its advantages but also came with responsibilities—being a legacy wasn't always as easy as it seemed.

"Who do you think you'll have for homeroom this year?" Ellen asked. "Death Breath? Barn Yard?" Ellen knew all of the teachers' nicknames—they hadn't changed much since *she* was a Wally.

"That's as easy to answer as who'll win the award for Best Liplock." Parker couldn't begin to worry about teachers—there was enough to stress out about already. "I mean, you can make an educated guess but you don't know for sure until your name is called."

Ellen rolled her eyes at the remark.

"Did you see my note?" Ellen nodded at Parker's laptop, an ultra-slim, 17-inch, top-of-the-line Orion notebook in a hot pink protective case. "I sent it last week."

"I'm...not sure." Parker lied on the grounds that the truth may incriminate her. "I'm so backblogged it's not even funny."

Ellen rested her hand on her hip and raised a suspicious eyebrow. She took a deep breath, surveyed the messy room once more, then puffed out her cheeks like she was about to deliver some earth-shattering news.

"Eighth grade is a tough year, Park," Ellen warned for about the hundredth time in a month.

Like I need to be reminded.

At Wallingford Academy, eighth grade was the most important year of school (understatement), and very possibly of your whole life (seriously). When you thought about it (which Parker did several dozen times a day for the last three years), it was the last time in your life you didn't have to stress about the big stuff: directed study proposals, application deadlines, dieting for prom, dieting for college, dieting for glamorous fundraisers...*adulthood.* On the other hand, it was the year when who you *were*—and who you ever *would be*—was pretty much set in stone. Success or failure hinged on the tiniest moments, the smallest details. Long story short? If you ruled eighth grade, the rest of your future was pretty much golden.

"And I know the possibility of leaving isn't something you really want to talk about, sweetheart," Ellen said gently. "But we have to talk about it eventually."

Parker closed her eyes tightly and tried to push the painful thought away. It was easy to pretend they were just like everybody else, but they weren't. The big house, and everything in it, was all they'd inherited from Parker's grandmother when she'd died. And an antique chair or a crystal wall sconce didn't pay the tuition at Wallingford; Ellen did. They weren't poor, but compared to Parker's friends, they might as well have been. Parker had always known that Siddie's remodeling gig would be over one of these days—and one of these days was getting closer and closer.

"We're okay on taxes for now. That should take us through the fall," Ellen said. "So at least we have that."

The fall? Parker tried to picture where that would get her.

"You could sell my furniture on eBay," Parker suggested. "I don't really need it." She tried to look sincere but it was hard sitting there on her canopy bed leaning against her goose down pillows. Frankly, she looked like someone who needed furniture.

"I hate the idea of leaving as much as you do. I know how hard it will be." Ellen smiled. It was a sympathetic-mom smile, the kind moms give you when your goldfish dies. "I just want things to be perfect for you, Parker."

"Things *are* perfect," Parker assured her. "Absolutely, totally, unbelievably perfect." She thought about school and her friends and the bottom nearly dropped out of her stomach. "I *need* this year, Mom. I've been waiting forever for it."

Ellen smiled again. This time it was the I-was-your-age-once smile. "You just promise me you'll make the best of whatever time you have left at Wallingford. There are great opportunities there for you," she said. "And you shouldn't waste a second of it on things that don't matter. You hear that, Park?"

Parker resisted the temptation to pull out an enormous pair of aviator sunglasses and hide behind them until the next century. "I wasn't planning on wasting anything," she reminded her mother. *It's me, remember?*

Ellen stood up from the bed and buttoned her suit jacket in Parker's mirror. "And who knows…maybe Siddie will want to rip everything out and start over."

With any luck.

Ellen reached over and kissed her daughter's forehead. "You're sure you don't need me to move my meeting?" she asked.

Parker shook her head. "I'm fine."

She could smell the lingering gardenia of her mother's perfume. The sweet and familiar scent always made her feel happy and sad at the same time—like looking at an old photo album or winding up the music box beside her bed.

"Everything will work out, sweetheart." Ellen folded the pashmina back into a proper square and placed it back on the shelf in the closet where it belonged. "I know it will."

"Me too," Parker said as her mother walked out. She called out in a clear voice, confident, cool, and on top of things, "Say hi to Siddie for me!"

Chapter 2

*P*ARKER STOOD AT THE foot of her bed and studied the clothes she'd laid out for the next day. After the exhausting morning of work, the look was finally coming together.

A uniform could say a lot more about you than most people understood. If the kilt was just a few inches too long, for instance, you might as well eat lunch in the social donut hole of the East Alcove. Or if your button-down shirt was too silky and tight then everyone assumed you went to Our Lady of Fatima Catholic School because that's how they wore them there. And if you got your blucher mocs from Value City Shoes…*hello,* people could tell.

Image counted if you wanted to be the best, and Parker got that, maybe more than anyone at Wallingford Academy. She wasn't the prettiest girl in class, or the smartest, and certainly not the richest, but there was no doubt about it—this was eighth grade; she could finally be as high up the populadder as she wanted to be.

The secret was pretty simple—wearing the right clothes wasn't as important as how you felt in them. Being beautiful was about what you did with what you had. Popularity was like that too—it was all about attitude. You had to picture who you wanted to be and then just imagine that's who you already were.

Parker opened her jewelry box and placed her Tiff's locket at the spot where her neck would be then added a delicate pair of silver earrings she'd gotten in Vineyard Haven over the summer. The cashmere pullover she'd decided on was new and oversized just enough to hang flawlessly down her back, but not so big to scream XXL. The button-down shirt she'd picked out was crisp cotton, white as teeth, and so starched it could have stood up and gone to school by itself.

She held the sweater up to her chest and put her hand lightly on her hip. It was her magazine cover pose (or Academy Award acceptance pose, whichever came first). Her skin was tan from a summer at the beach and her hair was loosely curled under from the morning's blow-dry with a thermal boars-head round brush. An extra swipe of bronzer powder along the bridge of her nose made it look smaller than it was. And the classic, regulation colors of the Wallingford uniform went well with her coloring (that was just luck, not work). Altogether, the look said confident but not stuck-up, pretty but not self-obsessed, excited but not super-anxious about it. *Although would staring at myself in the mirror for twenty minutes make me stuck-up or merely demonstrate my commitment to excellence?*

Parker set the pullover back down on the bed and opened her laptop.

It didn't take an Einstein to know that the care and maintenance of one's Facebook profile was essential to assuring a top position on the populadder. And it wasn't the *quantity* of time that mattered; it was the *quality*. There were new albums to add, Friends to confirm, photos to tag, groups to join, and countless invitations to RSVP to. Good manners were crucial—especially online.

And then there was the time-gobbling task of sorting through the people you may know section, which changed daily. (This was always the creepiest part, Parker thought. How did Facebook know that she knew them?) It was a necessity to continuously update and polish her profile—how else could people ever get to know the continuously updated and polished Parker Bell?

Parker tagged a few photos and sorted through the last of the morning's Friend requests, confirming seven new ones and ignoring some guy who lived in Paraguay. She looked at the final thumbnail photograph for the third time this week and the only hopeful Friend still waiting for an answer. She clicked open the pending request for the third time this week.

Ellen Bell—0 mutual friends

Her own mother! It was mortifying.

Why do they let mothers have their own profiles? Parker shook her head. It was something she would never understand. (Facebook should have a mandatory retirement age, she thought.) She left the pending request hanging out there in Facebook limbo and clicked back to the home page and to the toughest assignment of the day.

What's your status right now?

Parker twirled the silver friendship ring on her finger and wiggled her toes, now freshly pedicured a pale ballet pink. She only had a few minutes left before she needed to run out to meet her friends but she had to let the answer come to her. Thinking too hard ruined it. Not thinking hard *enough* and you were cheating yourself and your Friends. But it was more difficult today for obvious reasons. Updating her status didn't usually make her this nervous. Parker bit her lip and tried to concentrate.

What's your status right now?

Parker is...

She looked at her reflection in the screen, flipped her silky hair over one shoulder and put her fingers to the keyboard.

Parker is...ready.

Yes. One word. Powerful. True. Telling. Plus, she felt proud of herself for resisting the temptation to add:

...sort of.

Chapter 3

The five rules of La Coppa Coffee Tuesday:

1. It must be Tuesday.
2. It must be at La Coppa Coffee.
3. You must bagsy the comfy couch even if it means resorting to ugliness.
4. 24-hour cancellation policy. No exceptions.
5. What's said at La Coppa Coffee stays at La Coppa Coffee.

*P*ARKER COULDN'T BELIEVE IT was *finally* the day before school started: the first La Coppa Coffee Tuesday of the school year. After seven years of waiting, eight if you count kindergarten, the moment had arrived. She was only minutes away from seeing her three best friends for the first time as *official* eighth graders. Parker walked quickly past World of Beauty, Baby Cakes Bakery, and Hemingway's Books. Wallingford Towne Centre was filled with so many Wallingford students that you could smell the new leather of everyone's shoes.

Her phone buzzed as she walked past the Orion Computers Retail Store and through the courtyard toward the coffee shop on the other side. The texts from her friends had been building up all morning. Her message box was in need of a serious purge.

> Wher R U?!

> M$ULkeCRz

> 5 mins L8

And they all signed off the same way. Always.

> LYLAS

Love you like a sister.

Initially it was just the simplest way for the four best friends to text good-bye, and then, one of them, Parker didn't remember who first, said it aloud—like a word:

"…Talk to you later. *Lylas.*"

After that, it became part of their vocabulary.

"…See you then. *Lylas.*"

"…I'm sooo excited! *Lylas.*"

It was easy to forget it was an acronym because it sounded more like a name. Singular: Lyla. Plural: Lylas. Together, they were a unit. Parker never screened their calls and they never screened hers. If you created a group, they joined it. If you sent them Links, they clicked them. When your wall was blank, they filled it. It was who they were and how they signed off. Sometimes they added a :-) or a ;-)) or a ~:->, depending on their mood, but Lylas always came first. In email. In everything.

Parker pushed open the door of La Coppa Coffee. The engraving on her new friendship ring glittered for a moment in the morning sun: *Friends Forever.* The silver band was more fitting, Parker thought, than the macramé bracelets they'd all worn since Pinecliff Summer Camp two years ago. (Plus the colorful string always broke off in the shower.) Her throat tightened. It hurt too much to think about leaving the Lylas but she was determined not to let any of it show. At least the rings would last forever.

The smoky smell of espresso beans filled the air.

"Lyla!" Ikea Bentley, the most punctual member of the group, got up from the comfy couch with Parker's half-caf venti mocha macchiato at the ready.

"Lyla!" Parker wrapped her hand around the hot cup and they exchanged a double-air kiss. Their ample layers of sheer Lipglass, sticky enough to conjoin them at the lips forever, kept them from avoiding contact. "*So* needed this," Parker thanked Ikea for the much-needed fix and quickly took a sip from the frothy top.

"No probs," Ikea said licking her upper lip (actually the secret signal that Parker had a foam mustache). She handed Parker a napkin and nodded once the 'stache was clear.

Ikea was pronounced I-*kay*-a, like the exotic African lodge where she was conceived, *not* I-*kee*-ya, like the unexotic Swedish furniture store.

Like Parker, Ikea was an Aristobrat. Her father, a former Yalie and the senior partner at Bentley & English LLP, was a Wally from way back. Mr. Bentley was the kind of attorney who got calls in the middle of the night from the crown prince of Dubai, the secretary of state, or billionaire computer mogul J. Fitzgerald Orion himself.

Mr. Bentley's goal in life (as in the only thing he ever talked about, as in the blank application taped to the refrigerator, as in the bumper sticker he stuck to the mirror in his daughter's bathroom) was for Ikea to go to Yale. Just like he did.

It wasn't much of a stretch—Ikea was one of the smartest girls at Wallingford (the smartest girl on the *populadder,* defs) and she already looked old enough to be on Court TV. She was also the only African American girl in the class, which was good for college applications, but also could be really annoying because people were always trying to match her up with Brooks Jenkins, the only African American boy. Brooksie was totally beneath Ikea in every way, which no one understood—Wallys could be so blind.

"We're loving the tote." Parker admired Ikea's new bag—a pink and lime patterned canvas with a teaberry bottom. *Lavishly complimenting the other person's new thing,* whatever it was, was one of the many Lylas Rules. "Très cute."

Even the tote bag itself was part of the Rules: *Designer handbags were out. Designer totes were in.* Of course, the Rules were ever-changing, constantly amended, reversed, and modified. And there were always exceptions.

"Your tote is très cuter," Ikea gushed. (Another Rule: *You have to say the other person's new thing is better than yours, even if you didn't really think so.*)

Ikea sat down in the leather club chair beside the comfy couch and fixed her glossy straight hair behind her ears. Today's outfit was sunny, and perfectly complimented her hazel eyes. Ikea loved sunny colors. Usually they were printed on canvas or cotton, embroidered with flowers and combined with some form of pink. She was preppy. Seriously preppy.

And not in a fakester way, like an Abercrombie Zombie or a Polo-poser. If it had a croc, a duck, or a Black Dog on it, Ikea owned it. If it could be made out of ribbon, monogrammed, or engraved—she bought it. And she never shopped in malls, or even fancy stores like Langdon's. She bought oodles from Maax in Nantucket, the Lilly's in East Hampton, and CJ Laing's in Palm Beach. Ikea was a purist. A total prepsicle. It was impossible not to admire her focus.

Parker untied her belt and slipped out of her trim, voile trench jacket. She hunkered down on the end of the couch and kicked off her ballet flats.

"You are so super-tan, Park," Ikea said, kicking off her own Eliza B. Horse & Rider flip-flops. "Hawaiian Trops. Totally."

"You think?" Parker looked down at her impeccably bronzed arms. "I don't understand why…I wore fifty the whole time in the Vineyard." Or maybe it wasn't *exactly* fifty, Parker thought; maybe it was more like a family-sized bottle of baby oil, some lemon juice, and a Fritz Bandeau tankini for weeks on end. Parker kept that to herself though—she didn't want Ikea to think she had tanorexia.

"Tribb is going to go crazy when he sees you," Ikea told her.

Parker tried to contain her excitement. It was important to keep a level head about these things. *Tribb* was Tribble Manning Reese III, the Wallingford Tigers star forward and team captain. Tribb was the kind of guy who put his hands in his pockets, locked his knees and looked really good, you know, just *standing* there. Total front cover of Hottery Barn.

Ever since Tribb and Parker fox-trotted together in Miss Portia's cotillion class last year, it was obvious that he would be her EGB (Eighth Grade Boyfriend). It was all planned out:

she would go to his practices, they'd flirt by the lockers before first period, IM for hours, and have their first kiss after the Tigers game against the Fox Chapel Acorns, the first major social event of the season. He'd even get the lowdown on the dress she was wearing to Fall Social so they could coordinate perfectly (he was pretty metro that way). He'd give her a gardenia wrist corsage. A single but fragrant flower. Always a classic.

No one was more perfect for Parker—everyone thought so.

Parker counted out the weeks until Fall Social—she'd definitely be at Wallingford until then. "I don't need to impress Tribb Reese," she maintained. "Plus, Tribb should love...he should love...what's on the *inside*." Parker nearly choked on her words. For the first time, eighth grade felt so *real*.

"Absolutely," Ikea agreed. "The inside is so important."

Parker took a deep breath—the kind that sucks the tears right back into your head before they have a chance to come out. She settled into the couch and sipped on the mocha mach, pointing to the visible spot of skin above Ikea's capris. "You should totally get a tattoo back there," she said. "Like a little fairy. Or the Japanese symbol for peace or something."

Ikea twisted her head around and tried to get a glimpse of her own backside. It wasn't hard to miss—everyone else at La Coppa Coffee saw it clear as day.

"I heard Brie Channing got a butterfly tattoo on her ankle," Parker relayed. "Her mother doesn't even know about it." She sipped. "Now she has to always wear knee socks. Even for tennis."

Ikea's jaw dropped.

"A tattoo? Can I do it?" Plum Petrovsky called, leaving the barista counter with a coffee as big as she was.

"Lyla!!" They all traded another round of air-kisses, carefully avoiding any tragic coffee or Lipglass mishaps.

"All we really need to do a tattoo is a needle and some India ink," Plum said.

And she would know—Plum nearly got expelled last year for piercing Missy Foxcroft's ears in the girls' bathroom. Even though Plum was a Legacy too, she'd faced expulsion from Wallingford a total of four times. Most were grievous misunderstandings, false representations, and one possible case of extortion (which couldn't exactly be proven, but couldn't exactly *not* be proven either).

Plum took a seat at the other end of the comfy couch, took the top off her cup and blew on the dark, steamy liquid. She pulled her tiny legs up to her chest and wrapped her arm around her knees. The top part of her scribble-print Chuck Taylors were folded down and held together by double laces.

Parker blinked at the engraving on Plum's new friendship ring: *Friends Forever*.

Plum's skin was smooth as porcelain, her short, glazed haircut had one sharp streak of Cherry Bomb red (well, *today* it was Cherry Bomb red) embedded in the bangs, and her brows were nothing short of red carpet ready. She was heir to the Out of This World cosmetics empire and the company guinea pig. She was always getting Milky Way facials, Sea of Tranquility paraffin masks, and Close Encounters of the Botanical Kind splashes. Plum always looked great and usually smelled pretty fruity. It more than made up for the fact that she still hadn't grown into her training bra.

But as much as Plum obsessed over an eyebrow, she thought that boys were entirely overrated. Thanks primarily to her younger brother Nico, Plum maintained that the male species were all smelly, splashed water on their toothbrushes instead of actually *brushing* their teeth, drew bloody skulls on everything they owned, never flushed the toilet (no matter what was in there), and recited the lyrics of rap songs instead of having real conversations. Boys, Plum felt, needed brat bribes just to act human. And Parker had to admit, she wasn't always wrong about this.

"But BTdubs, no way are we doing a butterfly tattoo," Plum told everyone. "Butterflies are way played out," she said.

Parker and Ikea both nodded; *Butterflies are way played out.* A new rule was born.

"Ike…" Plum sipped from her drink. "…you think your parental unit can keep me out of detention this year?" She phrased the question casually, like it was no biggie to ask Mr. Bentley something like that. "My grandmother is *so* making my mother send me to Our Lady of Fatima if I get another detention."

"…I don't know if he can do that," Ikea said nervously.

Mr. Bentley had recently been named Wallingford Academy's new Board President, a job that would require an untold amount of time nosing around in Ikea's bizness. It would take the pressure she usually felt about getting an A+ in just about everything in her life (which apparently was required to get into Yale), put a lid on it, and turn the temperature up to scalding. But leave it to Plum to see the potential in Mr. Bentley's appointment.

Ikea bit at the end of her grosgrain watch band and then moved on to her thumbnail. Parker found herself biting at her thumbnail too. She could feel Ikea's pain.

"Hello, darls!" Katherine "Kiki" Allen, the very first-of-all-time member of the Lylas (and *third* generation Wally), burst into the crowded coffee shop with an armful of shopping bags, a stack of British fashion magazines, and hugsies for everyone. "I am *so* knackered," Kiki puffed. "I had the most *beastly* time getting out of the house."

Kiki had just returned from a summer in London with a brand new faux-English accent and gi-normous credit card bills from Harvey Nichols and Patrick Cox. Kiki was a Eurochameleon—instantly influenced by whatever country she'd just been visiting. It was like the time she came back from Paris and had to put a "*la*," "*le*," or "*les*" in front of everything.

On the other hand, Kiki looked fabulouz as only Kiki could. She wore a pair of metallic flats, humongous Cavanna sunglasses, and Studio D'Artisan jeans that looked like they'd been painted on her. Celebrity hairstylist, Adee Phelan, had given her wide, blunt bangs that reached down to the tips of her eyelashes (so soon every Wally would rush to the salon for the same). And ignoring the Designer Tote Decree entirely, she carried all her junk in a Lariat handbag the size of a Volkswagen. It was the British "It Bag," Kiki had said. Everyone in London had one.

Kiki's mother, Bunny, had once been married to a Bulgarian Count. She still made her dinner reservations under the name "the Countess of Battenberg" even though the marriage had lasted only eleven days.

Her great-great-grandmother on her father's side was Eugenie Singer of the Alexandria Island Singers, and her great-grandfather was Thomas L. Allen, heir to the Allen Railroad fortune. Dr. Allen didn't seem to be a *doctor* of anything. And although he was always dressed in a custom-made suit and tie, read the *Wall Street Journal* cover to cover every morning, and had his own full-time driver, he never went anywhere in particular. He'd never had a job in his life.

Kiki even had her own Centurion Card, which meant she could've charged a small island if she wanted to: the best kind of situation for a shopaholic. She could've paid everyone's tuition and then some (not that Parker would ever ask).

"You bagsied the comfy couch during coffee hour?" Kiki asked, sliding in beside Parker with a cup of English Breakfast tea. "How smashing!" She checked her lipstick in the reflection of her phone.

"Ikea saved the couch," Plum said, "with her enormously *smashing* booty." She sipped and grinned wickedly, twirling her Cherry Bomb highlight around her finger.

"My booty is not smashing," Ikea protested. "I'm so not-fat, you guys…" She tried to turn around again to have another look at her rear end. "…Am I?"

"Not if your scale is metric," Kiki said.

Ikea smirked. "Women shouldn't be so obsessed with their weight," she offered, suddenly super-serious. "Girls already face so many pressures in today's media-saturated society." Ikea was a recent graduate of the GirlPower Self-Empowerment Program and believed in all this type of stuff now. (Ikea believed in a lot of things, Parker noted, none of which made her butt look as thin as it was at the beginning of the summer.)

"We all admire your fat activism, Ikea," Kiki said. "It's one of your most fattractive traits."

Ikea laughed in spite of herself. Plum pulled her notebook out and starting sketching Kiki and her cup of English tea. She tilted her head and crinkled her nose as she drew.

"I saw these boots on Bond Street," Kiki stated, turning the pages of *British Vogue* around for the group to see. "The Brits do everything first," she proclaimed. "Liam Davies is a legend. He *invented* style." She pointed to a picture of a pale, super-skinny English rock star and the glamboyant boots she'd apparently almost bought. "He's an immense ledge. Immense."

Ikea peered closer at the photograph. "I'm sure Liam Davies would want to be known for his *music* more than a pair of purple boots and black nail polish," she said.

"You don't wear purple suede platforms if you don't want to be known for them," Kiki responded.

"I just don't think you should judge people by what's on the outside. That's all," Ikea argued. "Clothes aren't that important."

Alarm bells started going off in Parker's brain.

"Well thank you very much for the fashion update, Lilly Pulitzer." Kiki eyeballed Ikea's splashy Jubilee print top.

Parker quickly closed Kiki's magazine before things turned ugly. Everyone was completely stressing out about tomorrow even if no one was saying so.

"We're not here to focus on anyone's fashion felonies," Parker reminded them. "Tomorrow is a very big day. There are a lot of great opportunities for us." Saying the words out loud made Parker's stomach flip-flop. Ikea nodded. "We need to focus on the things that really matter. Remember?"

"Like planning for dresses for Fall Sosh," Kiki proposed.

"Fall Social is *two months* away, Keek," Parker said. *Some people may not even be here by then.* "I mean…we're the leaders of the school now. *Noblesse oblige* and everything."

"From everyone to whom much has been given, much will be required," Ikea quoted, looking like she might break into some song from the spring play.

"I just want to eat lunch in the West Alcove," Plum said, concentrating on the details of her sketch, "finally."

"It's like our destiny," Ikea agreed.

"Just like *my* destiny is these completely *to-die-for* pair of open-toe snakeskin D'Orsay slouchies." Kiki couldn't help but look at the back of her magazine. "Total must-haves."

There was an awkward silence as everyone stared at the slouchy boots on the back cover. Having just commented on all thirty photos in Kiki's new album "The Shoes I Bought in London," it was difficult for everybody to drool all over yet another pair.

Kiki looked up from her dream booties. "What?" she asked the group.

"Oh…*nothing*." Plum said, flashing the Hairy Eyeball over at Parker. (Plum's shockingly glamorous Hairy Eyeball was famous the world over. She could catch a bank robber with that thing.)

"They're great boots, Keek," Ikea said. "Must-haves all the way."

"So Lylas, let's review the rules," Parker brought the conversation back to the key issue of the day. "Eighth grade is…" she began.

"The most important year of school," Ikea answered correctly. "Possibly of our whole lives."

Plum turned the page in her notebook, sat up as tall as she could, and read some of the new policies they'd come up with over the summer. "We will set an example…" Plum began.

"For the whole school to follow…" Ikea added.

"We won't snub anyone," Plum recited. "At least not in public," she clarified.

"We will be nice to the noofs," Parker said.

"Because it can be super-intimidating being a new person at a new school, *especially* Wallingford," Ikea continued.

Plum turned the page. "We will not let petty problems…"

"Or parental expectations…" Parker put her hand on Ikea's.

"Or polyblend fibers…" Kiki shivered.

"…get in the way of our goals," Plum read.

"We will never be tempted to wear Vamp nail polish again."

"Vamp is so over."

"Clear is the new Vamp."

"We will not commit Facebook faux pas."

"Or Tweet uncontrollably."

"And require a Twittervention."

"We will blow-dry or flat-iron every morning, even if it all looked fine the night before."

"And we will condition."

"And exfoliate."

"And we won't make anyone feel unworthy just because of their underpopularity but we will still assume the best seats in the auditorium and the Good Table at lunch because we've earned them."

"And the number one, never-broken rule…"

"Friends first," they said all together and clinked friendship rings.

Parker tucked her feet happily back up on the couch. "Eighth grade is going to be great," she said. "The best."

The Lylas finished their drinks and walked out onto the street in front of La Coppa Coffee. The sun was shining on the square. It still smelled like summer: honeysuckle and fresh cut grass and swimming pools and suntan lotion. Parker smiled.

Facebook had not lied. Parker Bell *was* ready.

Chapter 4

*T*HE MASSIVE DOORS OF Wallingford Academy were propped open for the first day of school. Herds of younger students brushed by Parker as they raced through. Fifth graders. Sixth graders. Seventh. Even the little Wally munchkins. There was so much they didn't know yet. The weight of her responsibility had never felt so real. She couldn't leave. Not now. There was too much to do.

The original Wallingford seal hung above the archway in the foyer. It was a royal blue crest with a gold griffin wielding a broken sword. The motto was written below: *Semper Veritas.* Stay true.

The school was over one hundred years old. Every hallway, water fountain, bench, room and patch of grass was named after the person who paid for it. It was impossible to remember whose stuff was whose—they all just blended together in one Ellis-Collier-Whitney-Frick-Danforth-Elodie-Smythe Memorial mess. The only name anyone remembered was J. Fitzgerald Orion II, and that's because the computer billionaire's advertising was in every high-end shopping center, and Orion computers, media players and smartphones were on everybody's desks and in everybody's pockets.

Everyone knew Fitz Orion, especially if you were a Wally. If it wasn't for Fitz, Wallingford Academy would have looked exactly like any other private school: the glossy walnut floors, the gi-normous chandelier in the foyer, the grand ballroom on the upper floor, and the three-story main auditorium with thirty rows of plush velvet seats.

But Fitz had something special in mind for the countless millions he'd donated: he made Wallingford the first "Smart School" in the world.

With the touch of a button, the headmistress could dim all the lights or play music everywhere or instantly change the temperature of the building. But that was just the beginning. Throughout the building there were hundreds of hi-def, 3-D Orion Super-Screens. The Super-Screens could change depending on the theme of the week: Ancient Greece or Biodiversity or Planet Earth. They could also be set to Waterfall or Christmas Scene or Fall Social Decorative for less bookish events.

Orion kiosks had strategically been put up throughout the premises. You could check your homework assignments on them, see Live Feeds from any classroom ("Spy Feeds" as Parker and the Lylas called them), or watch a previous webisode from the eighth grade webcast, *Wallingford Academy Today* (which everyone did for a laugh even though nobody admitted it).

Chalkboards and whiteboards didn't exist anymore—instead the teachers used Orion Genius Tablets. No bigger than a paperback book, a Genius Tablet was the "control board" of the classroom. With the flourish of a Genius Pen, the teacher could project his or her notes on the Super-Screens, tests could be administered, and information logged and stored for years to come.

Wallingford was like the Home of the Future in Tomorrowland at Disney World. Sometimes it was pretty cool. Sometimes it made you nauseous. (Particularly if your own personal Tomorrowland was in limbo like Parker's.)

• • •

Parker darted through the foyer and headed straight for the first floor girls' bathroom, aka "La Cachette"—the hideaway, dubbed so by Kiki during last year's aren't-the-French-so-completely-fantabulous phase. Hardly anybody went into La Cachette because it was next to the Wally Munchkin class-rooms and it didn't have an Orion kiosk in it to Spy Feed on people. (The Lylas didn't Spy Feed unless it was a serious life or death kind of sitch.) It was also the least user-friendly bathroom in Wallingford with only two stalls, neither of the locks functioning (possibly the work of Plum Petrovsky, an Allen wrench, four bobby pins and a drop of Elmer's glue, but nobody could say for sure).

Plum was fixing Ikea's lip liner.

"Your vermilion margin is all wrong," Plum insisted as she artfully lined Ikea's mouth in pale mauve. "It takes away from your eyes, Ike. Your eyes are your main feature."

Parker sat down on the dainty chair beside the sink and stared at Plum's steady hand until her nerves settled. (Who knew that lip liner could be so relaxing?)

"I yove your yew yweater, 'arker!" Ikea said without moving her lips. "It's yrès yute."

"Yours is yrès yuter!" Parker joked back as she checked out her no-makeup-look in the mirror. She wondered how *her* ver-milion margin looked, whatever that was.

"OMGasp!" Kiki flew into La Cachette, went right for a stall and didn't even shut the door. "I just saw Tinsley who just saw Cosima who heard from Brie who just heard from her brother…" Kiki flushed the toilet with a push of her foot. "That Tribb is totally asking Parker to Fall Sosh…" She washed her hands, fluffed her hair, and sat up on the counter. "Which means we need to start shopping for a dress—like *yesterday*."

Kiki's hands were flapping up and down by her shoulders so fast that she looked like she might take off. It was a move the Lylas (including Kiki herself) called "the Birdie." Just the mention of Tribb's name made Parker's face turn bright red.

"Guys don't think about that kind of stuff until like the day before," Plum said, pulling a linen hand cloth off the neat stack by the sink. "That's just the Gossip Vultures circling around their next meal." She dabbed the corner over Ikea's lips.

"Maybe he's pre-planning," Ikea said. "Which is super-cute."

Parker was barely listening. She was thinking about Tribb and the first kiss and the coordinated outfits and the gardenia corsage. She was crossing her fingers and toes. She was making a secret wish.

"You okay, Park?" Plum asked as she put away her beauty tools.

Parker gulped down and tried to say something that might make sense but nothing came out.

"She's okay," Kiki said pulling out her sunglasses and fitting them snugly on her face. "Aren't you?"

"But of course." Parker spiraled her hand in the air and smiled. "It's me, remember?" The Lylas stood side by side in front of the mirror and took a moment to breathe. "Okay," Parker said. "Let's do this thing."

Chapter 5

$\mathscr{P}$ARKER ADJUSTED HER TOTE high on her shoulder so she could walk down the hallway toward the eighth grade lockers without ruining the full effect of her outfit. She walked first (kind of a rule but not really official or anything), Kiki second, Plum third, and Ikea last.

Friends were everywhere.

"Parker! Kiki! Plum! Ikea!"

Everyone shouted their names in unison. Parker's head turned left and right. The syllables started sounding like something you could dance to—the chorus of a Gwen Stefani song.

Avery Bitterman came up and threw her arms around Parker. "Love the tan! *Real*...of course!"

"Great new backpack, Aves!" Parker made sure to sound really excited even though she and Avery weren't exactly best friends or anything. "Très cute."

"Double smiley-face," Ikea added.

"Really?" Avery's own smiley-face brightened. She'd gone up a notch on the ladder just from that. "Thanks, you guys."

Duncan Middlestat didn't say hello even though he clearly wanted to. After getting his braces off at the end of last year, Duncan was poised to move into the upper third of the popu-ladder, although he didn't know it yet. He still thought of himself in a lower tier; it would take him a while to mentally catch up to the physical improvements. But he was definitely headed in the right direction.

"Dunkers!" Plum said. "Hawt new jacket!"

"It's *smashing*." Kiki's compliment sounded like it was delivered by Buckingham Palace.

"Really?" Duncan looked down at his sleeves, clearly baffled. (Boys were slow: an unfortunate fact of life.) "This is the same jacket I had last year."

"Must be just *you* then, Dunk," Parker said.

"Courtney! Tins! Natalie!"

"OMG!" Parker's fourth best friend, Courtney Wallace, her fifth best friend, Tinsley Reardon, and her sixth best friend, Natalie Taylor came over: hugs all around.

Courtney gave Parker the limpest squeeze of the bunch. "I am *so* completely embarrassed I forgot to tag you in that photo from my party last year, I'm really glad you picked up on it," she said, her voice sadly dripping with fakeness. "My bad."

"No biggie." Parker forgave her. "It wasn't the best photo of me anyway."

"That's what I thought." Courtney smiled.

"Great 'do, Tins!" Parker remarked.

Tinsley's hair was looking even more volumized than usual.

Tinsley tightened the fancy barrette in the back of the pouf on top of her head. "It's a Hollywood Hair Bumpit." She let the Lylas have a peek of the plastic insert underneath her hair. "*Way* more volume than just the regular Bumpit."

"Nice," they agreed.

"*Pouffy.*"

"Sweet bangs, Keek!" The Hyphenators, Cosima Adrianzen-Fonseca and Emily Crawford-Green, admired Kiki's new hair—the must-have haircut that every girl at Wallingford would soon get, according to Kiki.

"Yummy sweater! Fabulouz glasses! Loving the turtleneck! Cute scrunchy!"

Per the Rules, the Lylas found something to like about everyone. The walk to the lockers was going even better than Parker had imagined.

Plum tugged on Parker's tote and nodded her head toward an unfamiliar girl standing by the water fountain. It was a Wally noof, nearly unheard of in eighth grade. Most people changed schools earlier on or waited to be freshman—eighth was *the* harshest year to change schools.

Parker gulped.

The new girl had a quilted Coral Vines tote dangling from the crook of her arm and a matching headband holding back her long curtain of baby-blond hair. Her eyebrows were a deep shade of brown, though, and still in their natural state, enough to make Plum's fingers twitch for tweezers and some eyebrow gel. She bent down and took a drink from the fountain. Parker could see the colorful macramé bracelet that fit loosely around her slim wrist. It was just like the ones the Lylas didn't wear anymore.

"Who's that?" Ikea whispered.

Kiki peered over her sunglasses. Parker averted her eyes.

"That's Cricket Von Wielding," Tinsley Reardon answered loudly. She took out a Lipglass and twisted it open, smoothing on a fresh shiny layer. "We're loving the Coral Vines tote, right?"

"As in *Governor* Von Wielding?" Ikea gasped.

"Apparently the family wanted to find a school closer to the Governor's Mansion." Tinsley doled out the tidbit of insider info about Cricket like it was just the beginning of all that she knew. "Plus Swiss boarding school is so politically incorrect."

"I totally would have voted for Governor Von Wielding if I was eighteen," Ikea said. "The governor's platform really supports the African American and Hispanic agendas."

"My father doesn't trust the Democrats," Tinsley said. "But Cricket seems super-sweet. Don't you think?"

They all stared at the girl at the water fountain even as they tried not to.

Plum squinted. "Somebody should tell her about those eyebrows." She caught Parker glaring at her. "You know…" she added, "to be helpful."

Cricket Von Wielding hoisted her Coral Vines tote up over her shoulder. Parker waited to introduce herself but the new girl didn't look their way. She walked right past them, coolly pretending as if she hadn't heard a word or noticed them noticing her.

"So who do you guys think will get stuck with producing this year's webcast?" Tinsley asked, changing the subject.

Parker had actually forgotten completely about it. She never wasted energy thinking about completely lame-o things like the eighth grade webcast. It was like toothpaste or something—it was right there in front of your face all the time but who gave it much thought?

"Allegra Elephant and the Einsteins," Kiki speculated. "Obvz."

"Everyone knows it'll be Allegra Oliphant," Plum concurred. "She's been taking communication classes for *two years*."

"And she has absolutely no profile," Tinsley commented. "No Friends whatsoever."

"Except the Einsteins," Plum said.

Tinsley tried to contain her snicker.

"It will give Allegra something meaningful to do with her year," Ikea said.

"It's not like she has anything else to shoot for," Tinsley added.

"Except the National Debatathon Championship finals," Kiki muttered.

"I'm actually *psyched* for Allegra," Parker said.

Everyone except Tinsley smiled. "Totally," the Lylas agreed.

• • •

The eighth grade locker area was perched above Wallingford's north campus. It was easy to gaze out the windows to see last year's eighth graders starting their lives out as Wallingford High School freshman—a glimpse into what Parker's future wouldn't be. It was close enough to make anyone forget their combination.

Parker found her new locker and opened it up. The eighth graders got double-deckers instead of the pointless half-lockers that barely fit anything. It was an administrative acknowledgment, Parker thought, that eighth graders had more stuff (which they did). Her locker would need some serious accessorizing ASAP. She envisioned some super-cute magnetic hang-ups, colorful basket organizers, a little mirror and corkboard, and multi-level shelving. A well-organized locker mattered—she didn't care what anyone else thought.

"Hey."

Even though Parker's locker door was blocking her view, she would recognize Tribb's voice anywhere. It was deep and the tiniest bit hoarse, like there was something a little bit bad behind all that good.

She shut the locker door and there he was. Taller and more muscular than last year…which made sense, as he was the oldest boy in class: nearly a year older than everyone else. He was beautiful in the most guy-like sense of the word. Parker wished she had a pause button so she could linger on him for a while.

"Hey." Parker leaned back against the locker, flashed a little smile, and made a swift scoop of the hair so that it fell gracefully back down on the face. (Full disclosure: she had practiced her "Hey" routine a dozen different ways in the mirror and this one seemed like the best.) She tried to ignore the chills creeping up from her toes. Parker wanted Tribb like some people wanted to be first in line to buy the latest Orion gizmo. It *had* to happen between them this year.

Tribb checked to make sure the collar of his polo was popped up. It was.

Parker could see the Lylas out of the corner of her eye. Ikea had the Birdie going and Plum had her arms wrapped around her own body and was smooching the air romantically. Meanwhile Tribb's teammates, Beaver Krieger and Kirby Vanderbilt, were standing directly behind Tribb acting cool. Kirby wasn't nearly as cute as Tribb. He looked kind of like a big bird. A big bird with hair and teeth…and a popped up collar. But Kirby was nicer than most of the Tigers and he always got a good part in the spring play, which meant a lot of girls liked him. And Beaver was, well, *Beaver*. It wasn't his nickname for nothing.

Kirby caught Plum's make-out sesh with herself and started giggling. Plum quickly stopped.

"So…" Tribb nodded.

She waited.

"So…" Parker said coolly.

"Really big lockers this year," Tribb said.

"Yeah." Parker looked inside the tall metal box and twirled a piece of her hair. "Crazy-spacious."

"You could practically live in there." Tribb laughed. *He was so ridiculously cute when he laughed. Serious faint alert.*

"It's like nearly an apartment!" The comment came out oddly high-pitched. Parker tried to keep breathing. They both stared into the empty locker for a while until it seemed like that particular bit of conversation had run its course. She let Tribb make the next move.

"So—the *big year*…" Tribb said. "Eighth grade. Pre*tty* weird."

"The *big year*…" Parker answered. "Really we*i*rd."

"So we should, you know," Tribb said, "like hang out sometime."

"Yeah. No, *totally*," Parker agreed. "Hang out. Definitely."

"Sweet." Tribb nodded.

"Completely." Parker smiled and batted her eyelashes twice. (Twice was the perfect number for a moment like this.) *Am I breathing? I can't actually tell.*

Tribb motioned to his friends that it was time to go. "So see ya around…Parker."

The three of them walked down the hall toward the classrooms.

"You too…" She answered back cutely. "Tribb."

By the time Tribb and his friends had disappeared, Parker had no air left in her lungs to make sound. The whole conversation just echoed in her head. She tried to replay all the best parts so she'd remember them.

The Lylas had gathered around Parker's locker.

"Your first EGB moment," Ikea swooned. "That was *so* unbelievably romantic."

"That was *so* unbelievably ridiculous," Plum mumbled.

"Was I too primpy?" Parker looked at her reflection in Kiki's sunglasses and fixed the front part of her hair. "I mean, you guys would tell me, right?"

"You were immense," Kiki said. "*I* wanted to go out with you."

"Like, if you were Tribb and I was me," Parker adjusted her sweater, "you wouldn't think I was a total idiot?"

"Not at all," they agreed.

"You were great, Park," Ikea assured her.

"And the hair scoop thing was really well executed," Plum added. "Sweet."

"But not too *too*," Kiki agreed.

Parker shut her eyes and tried to shake out her nervousness. *Through the fall—I can make it all happen by then.*

The first bell rang. Parker smiled. She and Tribb were now officially a couple. All was going according to plan. Now if she could just use this nice bit of information to convince her mom that this made it absolutely *impossible* to move, she would be set.

Chapter 6

$\mathscr{P}$ARKER MANAGED TO MAKE it through Mrs. Bernard's European history, Winkle's biology, and French II with Guertner. Eighth grade, however wild it seemed a few hours ago, was now dull as dirt. Tribb wasn't in any of her classes except Virtual (aka *online)* Humanities, which sucked for obvious reasons. And Kiki was her lab partner in Winkle's class, which meant that Parker would be dissecting all the stuff herself.

Classes were driving Parker nuts. Eighth grade wasn't about being stuck in a room. And her tan was fading by the second. She'd practically be a ghost by lunchtime. Time was flying by and nothing was done.

Fourth period, Cricket Von Wielding committed a major party foul by sitting in the choice seat in A.P. English (third from the front, window side). But Parker took it in stride. This was a new school for Cricket, she reminded herself. Cricket had probably been perfectly happy where she was. Popular. Comfortable. She'd probably had a best friend. *Or three.*

Parker walked to the next best seat, sat down and organized her stuff. She put a hand ever-so-lightly on Cricket's shoulder.

"I just thought I'd introduce myself. I'm Parker Bell," she said brightly. "And I'm loving the tote." Parker pointed to the Coral Vines. "Très cute."

Cricket nodded and blinked. She conveyed no truly recognizable emotion. Parker thought it must have been shyness. Or paralyzing insecurity. According to Gurl.com, "Insecure people often show no recognizable emotions."

"And I just wanted you to know," Parker told her, "that if there's anything, *anything* at all, I can help you with, don't be afraid to ask." Cricket gathered her hair up into a ponytail with her hands then let it go again. Her curtain of blond hair fell down against her back. "It can be really super-difficult being at a new school and not knowing anybody," Parker went on, putting herself in Cricket's shoes. "But now you know me!"

"Thanks," Cricket said with a tiny nod.

Mrs. Acklin sat down at her desk, took out her Orion Genius Pen and Tablet.

"And BTdubs," Parker whispered again, "you're totally invited to Friend me. I'll definitely confirm you." Parker nodded and waited for a reaction. *I mean, Friends from day one—that's a serious advantage for a noof.*

"Good to know," Cricket replied.

"*The…Elements…of…Style…*" Mrs. Acklin wrote the title of the first chapter on her Tablet. The words instantly appeared on the Super-Screen in the front of the room.

• • •

Until Friday, eighth grade wasn't much different than seventh or even sixth grade, Parker thought.

Plum had made it through the week without getting any yellow slips despite the fact that she had a concealed sewing kit in her tote and was chewing gum. (She usually just stuck the gum over her teeth like a custom-designed watermelon-flavored retainer. No one got yellow slips for retainers.) She had tried to lay low and avoid Death Breath, the Medieval Literature teacher, the Grim Reaper of detention.

Ikea had bagsied the corner seat in the back row of Advanced Technologies. She didn't have to pay a ton of attention because she'd already taken Pre-Advanced Technologies last spring and she knew the first three chapters by heart. She'd looked around the classroom and had taken a count, she told Parker. African Americans made up 13.4% of the American population, so why weren't there 53.6 black kids at Wallingford?

And someone had the brilliant idea of putting Kiki and Kenneth Accolola in every single class together. Neither of them would learn a thing all year—they'd just discuss the pros and cons of kitten heels verses wedges and argue about which celebrity "Wore It Better" in *InStyle*. Quel else was new?

But Fridays were different. *Why?* Because the much awaited and highly anticipated *Matin* was on Friday.

• • •

Like "La Cachette," "Matin" was a fancy name somebody invented for something fairly simple—the weekly Friday morning assembly. It was also the biggest populartunity of the week.

The Lylas met by the old row of phone booths in the opulent Freeman Foyer and did a quick Hair & Makeup check. Discounting the Duke Ballroom on the top floor, the Freeman Auditorium was the largest and grandest room at Wallingford. It had a huge chandelier, an orchestra pit, a Broadway-quality stage, twelve hundred velvet seats, a state-of-the-art concert hall sound system and the largest indoor Super-Screen of any prep school in the country, courtesy of Fitz Orion.

So a little extra blush was appropriate.

They all confirmed that Parker's tan was still visible—not as

Hawaiian Trops as the first day of school, but still really good. They popped a few cinnamint Tic-Tacs before they walked into the crowded space. (*Cinnamint Tic-Tacs before major events* was a really old rule.) And they reviewed the rule created years ago for today's event: *Assume the best seats in the auditorium because we've earned them.*

James Hunter, still the weirdest kid in the class, was manning the AV booth. Some people weren't even on the populadder; they just stood beside it like it didn't even exist—James was one of those people. Hardly anybody even knew his name except Parker. She'd had him as her maypole partner in kindergarten. Most people called him "that AV guy." He'd barely said ten words since maypole. Usually he just lurked around with his camera taking photographs of the lunch ladies serving up mashed potatoes or Madame Guertner buttering her bread. With his terminal case of bed head, dark faraway eyes, and never-ending silence, it was impossible to tell if James was truly emo or just thought he was better than everyone else.

The headmistress, Ms. Hotchkiss, made a humongous deal out of the first Matin of the school year. It was when she introduced new faculty members (yawn), announced changes to the Board of Trustees (double yawn), and appointed the new eighth grade production staff for the school's webcast, *Wallingford Academy Today* (too many yawns to count).

Hotchkiss made the webcast assignment out like it was the greatest thing in the world, but everyone knew it was social Siberia. She assigned the same eighth graders every year—the ones who were hallway monitors in fifth grade, on the Uniform Enforcement Committee in sixth grade, and on the Green Team for Garbage Reduction in seventh. In other words, the

Wallys who began obsessing way too early about how their extracurricular activities would look on their college applications. This year that most surely meant assigning Allegra Elephant and the Einsteins, her overachieving friends. (Allegra had been waiting for this moment for years.)

Parker chomped the last of her Tic-Tacs and surveyed the lay of the land from the back row of the auditorium. Graham Henry, the sixth grade Wally whose claim to fame was burping the Alma Mater from start to finish, turned around and belched at the Lylas.

"Lovely, Chunder Cheese," Kiki remarked dryly. "How did you get to be such a disgustoid?" She rolled her eyes.

"How's my favorite daughter?" A deep, kettle-drum voice called out from behind them. It was Ikea's father, Mr. Bentley.

"Dad?" Ikea was surprised to see him there in person. He never did anything in person. She instantly started biting her thumbnail as soon as she saw him. "You came in for the announcements?"

"If something's important to my daughter, I make time for it!" Mr. Bentley did a quick check of his gold Roley.

"You do?"

"That's why I agreed to be board president," he said. "So I can be more involved in your day-to-day school life," he explained. "Make sure my baby girl gets into Yale. And not slough off…" Mr. Bentley pat Ikea's shoulder lightly like you might pat something you didn't know you were allowed to touch. "Like you did last year."

Ikea had one of Kiki's fake smiles frozen on her face. "Great," she said. "Thanks, Dad."

Ikea waved to her father as they walked away. She turned to Parker. "You're so lucky, Park," Ikea whispered. "I would do anything not to have him breathing down my neck all the time."

Parker smiled and held on tightly to her locket. It was nice of Ikea to say, but Parker never felt lucky about that.

The auditorium was noisy. The chatter bounced around in the three-story space. The Lylas walked down the aisle past hordes of younger Wallys toward the eighth grade section in the front.

"*Aristobratshmshshmsh. SssmssmArisotbrat.*" Parker heard the seventh graders whispering to each other behind her back. It was the same thing Parker remembered feeling at the beginning of last year watching the eighth graders take their places— but there was no reason for anyone to feel intimidated. Parker intended to live up to the responsibilities of her title.

Each year the most popular eighth graders inherited the back row of the section. The premier seat was closest to the aisle and then progressed downward from there. Only top tier people sat in the back row—the front was reserved for people like Allegra.

"Assume the best seats," Parker reminded them for the last time, "because we've earned them."

When they got there the row was filled, all but the first four spots closest to the aisle: the four best seats in the whole auditorium. *Yes.* Kiki slid on in acting as blasé about the impressive accomplishment as possible. As did Plum and Ikea. But Parker felt the warmth of the accomplishment wrap around her like a blanket. She couldn't help but smile. She was truly unstoppable.

Parker held her kilt and sat down onto the plush velvet.

"We're loving the new hair, Keek!" Laurel Posvar yelled from down the row.

"Thanks, darls." Kiki gave a regal wave. "It's such a cringe that I'm going to have to see my haircut on everybody sooner or later," Kiki mumbled to Parker. "I mean, it was my idea." She did her best to seem like she was actually dreading the thought of all the WannaKikis running around Wallingford with her haircut.

"Parker, you need to put up the vineyard pics on FB! ASAP!" Tinsley added. "We're dying!"

"I know! I know!" Parker smiled and made her crazy-busy face.

Kiki squinted. "Hey, isn't that Curkette Van Helsing down there sitting next to Court and Tins?" Kiki asked Parker.

Parker looked. "You mean *Cricket Von Wielding?*"

"Whatevs."

A noof in the last row? It was practically unlawful, inappropriate and at the very least, really confusing. *Good for Cricket,* Parker thought. *She's fighting through her darkest moments.* Tinsley and Courtney were admiring Cricket's headband (pink and lime green Piccadilly—matching today's tote).

Plum took out her notebook and started sketching and popping her gum. Tribb walked by them, and Parker fought back the butterflies. She squeezed the edge of Plum's kilt into her fist and tried to look in a different direction so Tribb wouldn't think she saw him first.

"Hey." Tribb nodded as he passed.

"*Oh...*Hey." Parker nodded back.

Tribb moved into a row near the front and sat down. (Boys never cared about the seat thing as much as girls did. Ikea thought it was biological. Plum thought it was typical. Kiki just thought it was weird.)

Ikea reached over and flicked Parker on the knee. "You guys are so massively cute together!"

"Yeah," Kiki said. "*Adorabla.*"

Kirby and Beaver sat down next to Tribb. Kirby turned

around toward Plum and looked like he was about to say something but then only cracked his neck, blinked, and turned back around.

"Retardis Involuntaris," Plum said to Parker as Kirby made his unusual collection of moves. "I think it's incurable."

The lights began to dim. The music teacher, Mrs. Rouse, sat at the grand piano. She lifted her fingers and began to play.

In the darkness, Parker looked at what Plum was sketching. It was a self-portrait.

"You're the best artist in the whole school," Parker whispered. Plum probably would have smiled if it wasn't for the hand suddenly thrust in her face, palm faced upward. It was Death Breath.

"Gum." Death Breath said before the room grew completely dark.

Plum spit her blue wad into the Medieval Literature teacher's palm. The fruity deposit was traded for a yellow slip that Plum stuffed into her shirt pocket.

"Lovely," Plum said as Death Breath sat back down across the aisle. "To add to my collection."

The teacher took out a napkin filled with other colorful wads of chewed gum and added Plum's to the top of the heap.

"Looks like you added to that collection too," Parker noted. They tried not to crack up but it was impossible to keep a few LOLz from escaping.

"*Shhhhh!*" Allegra Oliphant turned around and pointed. Her eyes were magnified through her thick, bright red glasses. Allegra didn't even care who she was shushing. Parker could relate. After all, this was Allegra's moment and no one was going to spoil it.

Chapter 7

*I*T WASN'T THE TOTAL darkness in the Freeman Auditorium or the flourish at the end of Mrs. Rouse's piano playing that shut everyone in the auditorium up—it was the purposeful and recognizable clip-clop of chic but sensible high heels as they made their way across the glossy wood stage. It was a sound that could belong to only one person: Hotchkiss. The sound alone (plus a touch of dehydration) had even made a fifth grader faint at graduation last June.

"Welcome to the commencement of the one-hundred-and-twelfth year of Wallingford Academy. We have a very special year in store for us indeed!"

Hotchkiss stood at her podium clutching her ever-present Orion Tablet. Hers was slightly larger than the teacher's and jet-black—the school's controlling motherboard. She pressed a button and the lights dimmed. She pressed another to illuminate the Super-Screens around the room. Her hand movements were as stiff as her well-coiffed hair (aka, helmet-head), and her voice didn't raise and lower like a normal person's—the words just floated out there above the podium, all strung together neatly, like her pearls.

Most Wallys called Hotchkiss "the Terminator" behind her back: living tissue over a metal endoskeleton—sent back from the future to destroy the world, one Wally at a time. Parker never found the theory all that unreasonable.

"I also have the great pleasure," Hotchkiss continued, "of introducing the new president of the Wallingford Academy Board of Directors, the Honorable Gardner H. Bentley the Third."

Hotchkiss waved her pen around the front of her Tablet and photographs of Ikea's father with gobs of super-important people soon surrounded the auditorium. Mr. Bentley held his suit in place and half-stood up for the mandatory applause, then checked his watch again. Despite what he said to Ikea, he seemed fairly ticked to be there.

Hotchkiss droned on with her yearly comatastic Welcome Back Wallys Address. *Intellectual development* this, and *embark on life's journey* that. She reminded the students that her door was always open.

Why did people standing at podiums always say the exact opposite of what was true? Parker wondered.

She glanced at Kiki, who was thoroughly enterdrained—as were most of the Wallys in the room. Only Allegra and the Einsteins were sitting at attention, nodding in agreement with everything Hotchkiss said. *Two words: Suck and Up.*

And then, for the moment nobody was waiting for: Hotchkiss waved her pen and the screens around the room rippled with the *Wallingford Academy Today* webcast home page. With another point of her stylus, a montage of the eighth grade producers from years past appeared.

Who were they? Who remembered?

Parker did feel sorry for them. They'd all wasted what could have been the most important year of their lives in a dark studio. But they probably didn't even realize it was wasted. They didn't have three-hundred-and-ninety-four Friends depending on them. Or a content-rich profile to maintain. Or meaningful

Tweets to Twitt. Or an Aristobratic title to live up to. They didn't need to get every moment just right because at any second they'd have to pack up everything they owned (including their Steiff teddy bear collection, an empty goldfish tank, and dozens of flannel pajama bottoms) and leave everything and everyone they knew behind.

Long story short? They didn't have a life to lose.

But Parker was actually happy for Allegra—it would be the best thing that ever happened to her.

"An enormous amount of thought and consideration went into this year's decision," Hotchkiss continued, staring directly at the Einsteins. "Fitz Orion, my good friend and esteemed alumna, was *personally* involved in this year's appointment."

Allegra smoothed out the pleats of her polyblend kilt.

"So it is my pleasure to announce this year's…"

"You wanna go to World of Beauty after school?" Kiki asked Parker with a yawn. "I need a new mascara wand."

"*Shhhhh!*" Allegra turned around. Even in the dark, her huge Hairy Eyeball gave Plum's a run for its money.

"*Shhhhh* yourself!" Kiki hissed back. "Jeeze la weeze."

"*Parker Bell…*" Hotchkiss announced.

Parker frowned. She was imagining things, right? At first, it sounded like Hotchkiss had said her name. But that was impossible. Hotchkiss *couldn't* have said Parker's name because she wasn't an Einstein and because it was the most important year of her life and because if she had, it would have ruined the entire plan. Hotchkiss couldn't have said her name. *Parker had things to do!*

Wallys everywhere turned to Parker and started clapping.

Everyone was moving in slow motion, their hands coming together and moving apart again.

Hotchkiss *had* said her name.

No. Wrong. Impossible. Parker Bell had *not* been assigned to produce the *Wallingford Academy Today* webcast: the Vortex of Darkness. It wasn't even noon on Friday and already her life was over.

"*Katherine Allen...*" Kiki was still set on stun-mode about Parker when her name was called. The info didn't compute—too many programs trying to open at once.

"*Plum Petrovsky...*" Parker's head was spinning. *All of us! All the Lylas!*

"*Ikea Bentley...*"

It was done. Hotchkiss had taken them all. Stolen them away to the dungeon like an evil child-catcher.

The slo-mo applause continued. Parker held onto her arm rests to keep from fainting. Allegra looked like she might fall right into the orchestra pit.

"And our technical staff," Hotchkiss called James from the AV booth. "*James R. Hunter...*" James looked shocked, the first recognizable emotion Parker had seen from him since his pinch pot exploded in the art room kiln.

"And *Leonard Schlaterman.*"

Kiki's head wouldn't stop vibrating. She looked like she might need temporary hospitalization. *McDweebs* Schlaterman. *Greeeat.* Parker could hear Kiki's faux British accent in her own head: "How utterly smashing."

Hotchkiss asked them all to stand. "The *Wallingford Academy Today* Staff!" she repeated.

The Lylas stood. Their faces instantly projected larger than life around the room. Mr. Bentley applauded. As did everyone in the audience.

Mrs. Rouse began to play and the Wallys sang. Parker could hear Graham Henry belching somewhere off in the distance.

Hail our Alma Mater, Wallingford we sing.
Cherished are the mem'ries, which 'round thy old walls cling.
May thy glorious spirit ever stay thy loyal ones,
And lead us to our future, with friends un'numbered come.
Then what e'er betide us, we will together stand,
By one bond united, common impulse grand.
Call us there together, while we raise our voices high,
O' Wallingford Academy, thy spirit cannot die.

Chapter 8

When in doubt, buy lipstick.

$\mathcal{S}$OME PEOPLE MIGHT EAT an entire box of Hostess 100 Calorie Twinkie Bites when they were feeling blue, or lounge around for days in Juicy velours. For the Lylas however, there was only one thing to do at a time like this: try on makeup at World of Beauty. Somehow everything always seemed better at the cosmetics counter. More, you know, *beautiful.*

"*Why?*" Kiki groaned in front of the mirror. "*Whyyy?*"

She wiped hot pink lipstick off her lips with a cotton ball dipped in makeup remover. It was the tenth or eleventh one she'd tried on. The residue of colors still hung around her swollen lips. It looked like she'd been kissing Popsicles.

"I think it's some kind of sick punishment," Parker said.

"She hates me, that's for sure," Plum said.

"Something we did in a past life maybe." Ikea thought.

"This is worse than detention," Plum said. "Detention doesn't last forever."

"My life is over," Kiki added to the cringe-fest.

"Urrrgh!!!" Parker tried not to scream her head off even though she wanted to (that generally should be done in private, two pillows over the face, inside the closet, behind some coats).

"I know. It's heinous…" Kiki whined. "*Beastly*."

"Pure torture," Plum agreed.

Kiki showed everybody the sleek, electric, self-curling, Anastasia mascara wand she'd been holding in her hand since they got there. It was the floor model and said "Try Me" on the side. It was the only one in the store. Honestly, the wand looked a little sweaty.

"This is absolutely *exactly* the mascara wand I've been looking for my whole entire life," Kiki lamented. "And Anastasia discontinued it!" she gushed. "*Why?* Why would you discontinue something so totally ultra-smash? It's complete and total crap. Pure torture—I agree with Plum."

"I know, sweetie. I know." Parker tried to be sympathetic. And she was. She really was. "But we were talking about the webcast assignment."

Kiki looked up. Her eyes were rimmed in the smudgy black of five different kinds of mascara. "Oh yeah," she remembered. "That's really beastly too."

With that, they walked silently down the eye shadow aisle. Zillions of tempting colors sparkled from their trays. Parker tried to get in the World of Beauty mood but she just couldn't. She pictured the Lylas sitting around in the dark studio with James Hunter and McDweebs Schlaterman. It was such a terrible waste.

"Can't we make up a new rule or something today?" Plum asked. "Like gladiator sandals are so out? Something like that?"

"I don't feel like it," Parker said as she opened up a multicolor eye shadow palette then clipped it shut again.

"But gladiator sandals *are* so out, Park." Kiki backed Plum up.

Ikea pulled out a clear Lip Venom and dabbed a teeny bit

on her lips. "You know there's only one new black person at school?" She sighed as she coated the gloss on thickly and looked in the mirror.

"There's an Indian kid, I think," Plum told her.

"Two Chinese," Parker reminded her.

"An Italian," Plum remembered.

"That doesn't count!" Ikea frowned. "Owww!" She yelped as the Lip Venom kicked in. She twisted the top back on the tester and shoved it back in its spot. "There's so much pressure on me to be perfect, you guys!" She wiped the evil lip junk off with a Kleenex and threw it away in the garbage, and then looked in the mirror to check and make sure the damage wasn't permanent. "You have to be perfect when you're black." She crossed her arms and looked away. "Perfect at everything."

"There's nothing wrong with being perfect, Ike." Parker put her arm around Ikea. She had no idea what it was like to be Ikea Bentley but she knew what it was like to be Parker Bell. She knew what pressure felt like.

"I wish I was as perfect as you," Plum said.

"No you don't." Ikea closed her eyes and pressed her hands over them.

The Lylas waited for a minute until Ikea felt better enough to start walking around again. Parker ran her finger along a row of eye pencils and wondered what Tribb was doing right that second. She wondered if he was thinking about her too.

Plum picked up a tester and smoothed some Minx Glimmer over her right eye with a Q-tip. Her left eye was already done, only it was a completely different color—Acid Rain. Ikea used the tip of her finger to smooth on a layer of Pale Ocean to match her eye color. Kiki just moped around in the mascara wand aisle with her face of many colors. When Kiki got on a serious whinge-binge like that, there was just no stopping her. They were all trying to process. Or avoid processing, whichever they each did better.

Plum sprinkled some iridescent sparkle powder on Parker's cheeks. "There," she said like that made it all better, like a little glimmer of makeup might give them their lives back.

But even World of Beauty couldn't make anything seem beautiful to Parker. They were the producers of *Wallingford Academy Today*. All the beauty had been sucked from her life. Royally.

• • •

"*How was school today?*" Ellen Bell stood outside the bathroom, attempting to communicate to Parker through the locked door.

"Fine." Parker was too bummed out for any more syllables than that, and certainly too bummed out for eye contact. She'd been in the bathtub for over an hour and it was nearly bedtime. Her fingers were all pruny and her ballet pink pedicure wasn't looking all that ballet anymore. Parker wondered how long a person could actually stay in a bathtub without completely turning to mush. Like that girl who stayed up in that tree all year in protest—couldn't Parker just stay in the tub? Couldn't *she* protest the injustice? Her friends could bring her food, and the toilet was right there.

"Are you liking all your classes?" Ellen asked.

"Yes." Parker gave the simple answer. Why wasn't her mother taking the hint and leaving her alone?

But that was the thing about mothers—they always knew when you wanted them to go away and that's exactly when they stuck around and kept bugging you.

"Death Breath still handing out yellow slips?" Ellen asked.

"Yup."

"I'm sure the new sweater was *fabulouz* as you girls say."

"Yeah." *Fabulouz.*

"I've been at Siddie's all day," Ellen rambled. "Some company rented out his house for the location of their new catalog, and I needed to move out a bunch of stuff. I think Sid just likes having people at the house. He certainly doesn't need the money."

There was a long pause. Parker took a deep breath and dove under the water. She opened her eyes and looked up at the ceiling through the shimmery stillness. She tried to drown out her thoughts with tub water. Tub water and a packet of Aveeno Bath Therapy that floated on the surface in bubbly chunks.

Parker couldn't hold her breath any longer. She popped up to the surface and gulped in the air.

"So you're trying to get the most out of school no matter what, right?" Ellen asked the loaded question.

"M'hm." *Oh yeah. Sure was.* Parker moved the warm water around in the tub with her hands.

"Great," Ellen said. "I can't wait to hear all about it."

Parker finally heard her mother walk back downstairs to put away the dishes in the kitchen. Cupboards open and closed. The coffee maker was set up for the morning. Parker grabbed a towel off the rack (Egyptian cotton, folded in thirds or else) and wiped her face. The outside lights turned off. The ice maker made ice cubes. Everything in the house went to sleep.

Chapter 9

$\mathcal{D}$ ESPITE THE HORROR OF their predicament, the Lylas bagsied the good table, as in *the* Good Table: West Alcove, by the windows, under the clock in the cafeteria. And Parker sat in *the* Best Chair at *the* Best Table: wall side, slightly off center, a view of everyone. She pushed around the macaroni and cheese on her plate and tried to think of a plan.

There were Super-Screens extending the length of the wall opposite their table. Joan of Arc was the theme of the day and the three-dimensional image across from them was of the young martyr tied to a tall pillar with flames lapping at her feet. It wasn't the most appetizing of themes for school lunch (most weren't) but the Lylas had had to witness all kinds of cruelty to finally earn their spot at the numero uno table. How bad was a little more gore?

There were only three tables in the West Alcove and you didn't dare sit there if you weren't A) in eighth grade, B) in the upper forth to fifth percentile of the populadder, or C) Kenneth Accolola. Kenneth got to sit there because he was Kiki's bezzie guy friend. He'd never be in the mainstream of Wallingford but it elevated his status by *a lot*. Kenneth was kind of a West Alcove mascot.

Kenneth flipped through the pages of *Us* and stopped on the "Who Wore it Better" page. He had his hand covering the answer. "Which one do you think, Keeks?"

Parker took a peek. She honestly thought neither celebrity looked very good.

"I'm going to say...*Amanda* wore it better," Kiki pointed to the celebrity on the left, "but that's not because I actually think Amanda wore it better...it's so obvy that Megan wore it better and that pairing that top with boyfriend-jeans is such a cringe..." Kiki chewed on the end of a carrot stick and waved it around like a Genius Pen. "But I think the sign of a true trendsetter like *moi*...and *vous*, Kenneth," she added, "is that people as in tune as we are always get it wrong." She crunched. "I think Megan wore it better, which definitely means *Us* mag picked Amanda."

Kenneth lifted his hand to reveal the answer. Kiki was correct. "You're so brilliant it makes me sick."

"I understand the audience," Kiki gloated.

"And she snaps her fingers in a *Z* formation!" Kenneth congratulated Kiki with a fancy wave and a snap.

Kiki finished her carrot stick proudly.

"Twenty-one, twenty-two, twenty-three, twenty-four..." Ikea pointed around the room.

"Stop counting white people, Ikea," Parker said. She regretted her lunch choice. She should have gone to the salad bar.

"I've lost count anyway." Giving up all hope, Ikea leaned on her European history book and finished her iced tea.

Sitting in the Good Chair at the Good Table, it was easy to pretend they were just having a normal lunch: Plum was adding a bikini top and cleavage to her self portrait, Kiki and Kenneth were playing "Guess the Designer" with everyone's handbags in the lunchroom, and Ikea was taking affirmative action while picking the tomato slices off her turkey sandwich.

But Parker couldn't stop thinking about the true terribleness ahead given their new roles as the Ambassadors of Bleh. The depress-fest was never-ending.

She could see Allegra and the Einsteins looking for a place to sit down. Allegra squinted through her thick glasses at the Lylas like she was plotting some serious revenge. Plum squinted back, protecting the whole table with her unique eyeball powers. Allegra. Plum. Allegra. Plum. A few more minutes of this and the entire lunchroom could have exploded.

"Shouldn't we ask them to, you know, sit with us, Park?" Ikea said it like it was the last thing on Earth she wanted to do but would do it anyway because that was a Rule. "Champions of the under-popular, and that kind of stuff?"

Parker thought about it but not so hard that she ruined any brain cells or anything.

"Maybe Allegra doesn't want to sit here," Parker said with a forkful of pudding. "The West Alcove can be a really intimidating place for most people."

"Yeah," Ikea agreed. "She'd probably feel better about herself in the main room."

They all nodded. They knew they were breaking a rule, or at least bending one, but there was a humongous difference between underpopular and painfully boring.

"Hey." Tribb stopped by the Good Table with Beaver and Kirby.

Plum quickly put her busty portrait away and gave Parker the secret signal for: "There's something in your tooth...no *that* tooth."

Tribb looked even cuter than he had last week. Fall Social was still two months away, but Parker could already picture it.

Tribb would show up at her house and she wouldn't quite be ready. He'd wait patiently at the bottom of the stairs like guys do in the movies. His heart would tumble when he finally saw her. He'd promise to bring her home by curfew but they'd still take a few extra minutes at the door. *Dot dot dot…* He'd look so unbelievably good in a tux, she thought. They'd look so good together.

"Hey," Parker said, discreetly scratching her right front tooth with her pinky. Mental note: *mani-pedi redo ASAP.* Second mental note: *think of more clever response to "Hey" than "Hey."*

Tribb leaned on the back of Parker's chair. She was only inches away from him. He smelled like Outdoor Fresh fabric softener sheets, which was like the ultimate thing a guy should smell like. (It was even on her EGB checklist she'd made last year, along with "dimple" and "taller than she was.")

"You coming to watch practice today?" Tribb asked her. At least two members of the Lylas, and possibly Kenneth Accolola, kicked Parker under the table. She didn't flinch but she could possibly have a bruise tomorrow.

"Don't you have a *Wallingford Academy Today* production meeting this afternoon, Park?" Courtney Wallace was standing right next to them with her lunch tray. She asked the question pleasantly, like she and Parker were second-besties or something. Courtney had always thought Tribb should be *her* EGB because they carpooled to St. Edmund's skating classes together in, like, second grade. And as Courtney had expressed on numerous occasions (though Parker had never asked her opinion), she and Tribb were more suited to each other. But everyone knew that prior to sixth, nothing counted toward EGB. And the "suited" thing was a Courtney-only opinion.

Kiki even explained that to Courtney in great detail in the form of an anonymous letter that appeared in the change pocket of Courtney's Vuitton folio wallet one morning.

The following Tuesday afternoon the vote came in on Courtney's petition to be one of the Lylas. Courtney Wallace would never be a Lyla, it was agreed. And Tribb would never be her EGB.

"Hey, Tribb," Courtney said as she twirled a pierce of her hair around her thumb.

"Hey."

"Why, we *do* have a *Wallingford Academy Today* production meeting, Courtney," Parker replied politely. "And that was so super-great of you to remind us. Thanks…" she said.

Courtney's new headband, Parker noticed, matched her new tote. And she was wearing a colorful macramé bracelet, which was so two-thousand-and-late. Courtney *knew* that macramé bracelets had been replaced by silver friendship rings (even though she hadn't gotten one). What was she thinking?

Parker's mouth was following the rules but her head was not. Her head was saying a whole bunch of other stuff to Courtney Wallace that was against a lot of rules. And not just Lylas ones. "But I can't *imagine* a production meeting is going to last so long that we can't come to at least the last part of practice," she said. "And the last part is really the best part. Right, Tribb?" Parker put her hand so close to Tribb's that they almost touched.

"Yeah." Tribb nodded. "For shiz."

Of course he totally agrees with me. That's the way boyfriends are.

"Double smiley face then!" Courtney shrugged and walked over to a table. "Oh, and I can't wait to see what the Lylas do with that webcast thingy," Courtney added from her spot. "I'm sure it'll be très cute."

"Thanks," Parker said with as much enthusiasm as possible (which was exactly zero). "We can't wait either."

"Is she being aggressive-passive, or what?" Kiki asked Kenneth under her breath.

Kirby leaned in and put his hand casually on the back of Plum's chair, just like Tribb had done with Parker. He didn't look nearly as cool though. He looked like he might tip over.

"That's my chair!" Plum said with a shove.

"Oh…oops…sorry…" Kirby quickly stuffed his hand back in his pocket and moved back behind Tribb.

"See! What did I tell you?" Plum whispered to Parker.

"So…" Tribb nodded. "Cool." He popped both sides of his collar back up equally again. It seemed like maybe one of their secret signals because Kirby and Beaver did it too.

Tribb smiled before he and his teammates walked toward the back exit. (*Dimple*, check! *Outdoor Fresh fabric softener sheet smell*, check! *Taller than she was*, check! *Totally, completely, perfectly hawt*, double-check!)

"He is distressingly fit." Kenneth gawked as they left.

"Distressingly," Parker agreed.

Part

II

Semper Veritas

Chapter 10

HERE WERE A FEW minutes in between Latin Studies and Expository Writing, so Parker stood in front of the Orion kiosk in the empty hallway next to the Munchkin classrooms. She was dying to Spy Feed on Tribb; she even knew what class he was in (Computer Skills) and where he was sitting (fourth row, window side), but that was impossible now. She couldn't afford to stalk Tribb between classes. There was no time to waste.

Parker held her breath as the cursor hovered over the *Wallingford Academy Today* archives folder. (Think presidential command center, nuclear bomb, and red glowing button.) She winced, then just sort of clicked it.

There were sixty webisodes in all—three years worth of Snoozeville. Parker clicked and watched and tried not to groan aloud.

How would someone even *describe* the webcast? she wondered. Think of a news show, a really boring news show. Then think of the super-early version of that really boring news show, the kind that might be on at 5:00 a.m. Since no one's really watching the super-early version of that really boring news show, the station puts the especially pathetic newscasters on it, the kind of newscasters that might pair beige with, say, off-beige, or do the kind of lame stuff that newscasters who make it all the way to the 6:00 a.m. broadcast would never be caught doing. *Then* think of something a thousand times more Retardis Involuntaris than that—and you pretty much have *Wallingford Academy Today*.

Each year, each webisode worked the same way. There was a "host" for each show, usually the fugliest member of that year's production staff and, almost always, the one with the worst forehead-height-to-face-size ratio. The unattractive (and forehead-height-challenged) host said hello and welcomed the audience the same way every show: "Hello, and welcome to *Wallingford Academy Today*." *Catchy!* That person sat behind a teacher's desk that had been painted beige to match the off-beige backdrop (remember the 5:00 a.m. broadcast?) so mostly the person just looked like a floating, poorly proportioned, head in a sea of weak mud.

Groan aloud!

Parker fast-forwarded through the depressing variety of academically important topics chosen, covered, produced, and starring each production staff member. The highlights in the archive included an inside look at that year's award-winning science fair entries: "The Science behind the Startling Reaction between Mentos and Diet Coke" and "The Genetic Basis for Migration in Monarch Butterflies Uncovered."

There were some regular features, like an interpretation of the Alma Matter by a musically talented Wally: piano or flute or even spoken word (no JK). And each show, one of the staff members stood in front of the beige teacher's desk and read the school lunch menu for the following two weeks—a completely pointless exercise since A) everyone could see the menu tumble forward anytime on the Orion Super-Screens, and B) nobody cared. Infamously, one Wally, Jeremy Landis, aka "DJ Jazzy Jeremy," actually rapped the menu. He became an instant cult hero (aka, nobody ever wanted to be seen with him again). Parker wondered if she'd ever be able to order turkey meatloaf with French fries again without thinking of Jazzy Jeremy doing the Worm.

In a word? *Wallingford Academy Today* was pathetic.

The show had no understanding of image. Parker spent more time each morning thinking about the effect her sweater choice might have on her audience than anyone had spent on the whole show in three years. She might as well have walked up to her mother with her suitcases packed and said, "Okay, I'm ready to start my horrible new life now. Take me away."

The webcast had only one subscriber—Arthur, the floor janitor. And the webisodes had barely been downloaded by anyone. The all-time high count was twenty-seven times for "Determining the Sex of the Common Bull Frog." Which apparently sounded a whole lot more exciting than it was.

Parker didn't even know how to produce something like that. None of them did. She was speechless.

The period bell rang. Wally Munchkins ran in from recess, hanging up coats and tossing snack-packs into their cubbies. Parker clicked out of the archives and back into Spy Feed so that if somebody went to the kiosk after her, they'd just think she was spying—not watching the webcast. Spying was way less humiliating. *If that's what Hotchkiss wanted, why didn't she just assign Allegra and the Einsteins?* Parker tried to think of a way not to worry the Lylas too much—they were all in their own classes and each had their own things to worry about.

• • •

Plum sat in front of her easel in Mr. Lewis's art class in the old bomb shelter in the basement. A box of brand new pastels was organized in a rainbow of colors at her side. Since it was the beginning of the year, all the pastels were still big and bright, not the little faded nubs of their former selves like they were by spring.

New pastels were Plum's favorite—inspiring her in a way that could have kept her drawing for hours. And she loved being in the old bomb shelter. The video cameras didn't work in there so no one could Spy Feed on you, and it smelled less like the waxy-lemon stuff Arthur used to shine the Wallingford hallways every night and more like turpentine, linseed oil, and wet paper pulp.

Arthur liked the bomb shelter too, Plum noticed. He liked hanging around in there and always ate his lunch in front of an easel.

Plum put her heart into her picture. Her arms were covered with pastel chalk. Even her face was striped from pushing away her hair with her colorful fingers. She was careful to keep her mouth closed so no chalk would get on her gum. She barely noticed Kirby Vanderbilt sitting at the easel across from her.

"It's good, Miss Plum!" Arthur whispered from the doorway of the room. He nodded to her drawing, which she'd only started. Plum smiled back.

Mr. Lewis looked up but Arthur had disappeared.

The art teacher had set up a still life in the center of the room. The fruit was plastic but you were supposed to imagine it was real. There were seven peaches and a silver jug set at different levels on top of a white tablecloth from the lunchroom. Mr. Lewis had spent the first part of class talking about the artist, Cézanne, and his subtle use of color and shape. He displayed Cézanne's artwork around the room on the HD Super-Screens.

Plum loved the pictures Mr. Lewis had shown. She could imagine being as small as a ladybug and walking in between the pieces of fruit the artist had painted. That's what she was thinking when she used her pastels.

"Neon orange?" Mr. Lewis asked from behind her. He said the word "orange" like it rhymed with "door-hinge." *Why did teachers always say words fancier than normal people?* "What about today's still life is neon 'door-hinge'?" He sounded suspicious.

Plum looked up at the teacher with her pastel-covered face, then back at her drawing. She didn't even realize she'd made the whole thing neon "door-hinge." She'd gotten lost in all the colors and just, um, kept going.

Plum shrugged.

"Your still life looks like a *discotheque*, Miss Petrovsky. One feels ill when one looks at it," he said. "Did you *not pay attention* to the lecture?"

"Yes…" Plum said.

"Yes?"

"I mean no." Plum corrected herself because it was a trick question. *Aha!* "No," she said clearly, "I did not *not* pay attention." She was confident. "I *did* pay attention."

"Then why does your drawing look like a…discotheque?" Mr. Lewis asked.

Plum tried to think of the right answer—she really did. But she felt like nothing she could say would be the right answer. She never had the right answer to teachers' questions. Plus she didn't even know what a discotheque was.

"I don't know," she replied.

"You don't know?" Mr. Lewis paused and looked at Plum's drawing again. "Well, when you have the answer to the question, Miss Petrovsky, please do come and tell me."

Plum slumped down in her chair. She wiped her bangs out of her face and popped her bubble by accident.

Mr. Lewis handed her a yellow slip. "I can ignore the gum, Miss Petrovsky, because I am a fan of the stuff myself," he said. "But not the blatant disregard for uniform regulations." They both looked down at the bright undershirt peeking out from the top of her shirt. All of her white undershirts were dirty this morning, but purple and white striped was maybe not the best alternative.

"Thanks," she said taking the slip. *Just what I always wanted.*

• • •

Ikea sat at the computer in the back corner of the Advanced Technologies classroom. She had her Asynchronous JavaScript and XML assignment open in one window, but she was more interested in working on a new glitter blinkie design for her MySpace page. She knew if she kept the AJAX assignment open in the background while she worked on her glitter blinkie, she could quickly click to her class stuff when Mr. Boliack came back into the room.

Ikea had gotten super-good at blinkie alphabets—her design generator was one of the most popular apps downloaded from her profile.

It was always funny to see how people used the lettering to suit their personalities. Suzanne Hoechstetter took Ikea's Diamond Dust design and wrote "Drama Queen" at the bottom of her profile with big, blinking stars on either side of the words. *Like Suzanne needed Flash animation to make that point clear to people.* Cosima Adrianzen-Fonseca turned the Cowgirlz Sparkle alphabet into her favorite quote: "To Live is to Dance and to Dance is to Live." Even Tribb Reese spelled out his name on his profile in her glittery Blu Lightning letters.

But this one was Ikea's best blinkie designs ever. She'd gotten the animation just right. It was so subtle that the letters really *did* look like they were made out of zillions of diamonds. She wanted to use it for something really special.

Be the change…

Ikea rubbed her eyes as she worked. Her eyes were bothering her. The optometrist told her that she could keep her new contacts in for longer than the old ones, but she thought these new ones were seriously uncomfortable. There were always trade-offs in this world. *Right?*

Be the change you wish to see in the world.

She finished typing the words. They shimmered on the screen.

"I like your blinkies." A new student walked by Ikea's computer monitor so quietly that Ikea didn't even have time to click back onto the AJAX assignment.

"Oh!" Ikea jumped. "I didn't see you!"

"No one here does…" The girl smiled and looked around at the chattering room of Wallys, sitting on each other's desks instead of working on the assignment. "I'm kind of invisible around here." Even covered in braces, the new girl's teeth were bright against her burnt-caramel-colored skin. "I'm Divya," she said with a small hand out toward Ikea. "Divya Venkataraghavan."

71

"I'm Ikea."

"I know who you are." Divya laughed. "Everyone in this school knows you." She smiled again and pointed to the sparkly words on Ikea's screen. "That's Gandhi."

"It's one of my favorite quotes," Ikea said. "I'm thinking about using it for my yearbook page."

"It's one of my favorites too," Divya told her. They both tilted their heads to the right and stared at the dazzling letters. "It's a good choice for the yearbook." Divya smiled and shook Ikea's hand. "It's nice to meet you."

"Nice to meet you too."

Divya shuffled back to her desk. Her kilt was nearly to her ankles, she wore dusty, brown loafers instead of the blucher mocs that everybody else wore, and her hair was longer and more beautiful than anyone's at school. But Divya was right—nobody in the room noticed her.

Ikea stared at the shimmery lettering on her monitor once more before she hit the return bar and typed:

Be the change you wish to see in the world
—Gandhi

• • •

"I *can't believe* I'm actually sitting in front of an Orion 2000 XZ, 27.9 gigs, Nova Core 4 Duo, 7400 GBs with Quartz Extreme eighty-two inch Cinema Display, four-trillion pixel capabilities and THX EX 360° surround sound!" Leonard "McDweebs" Schlaterman was standing in front of the editing computer with his arms outstretched like he just found land after being lost at sea for a hundred years. "Be still my heart."

Kiki rolled her eyes and propped her legs up on a spare

chair. She'd changed out of her brown school shoes and into the red Valerie Juene platform pee-toe pumps she bought in London. She hadn't seen them in days and missed them.

"I know, right?!" McDweebs murmured, not joking in any way.

The sad part? The only thing McDweebs loved more than the Orion 2000 XZ was Kiki. He was Kiki's boyfriend in second grade before she knew any better. There really wasn't a populadder back then so people like Kiki and people like McDweebs intermingled freely. They even got "married" (Major Secret. Embarrassing-city) with rings made out of green twisty ties and Bunny Allen's Schnauzer-Doodle, Snickers, as the flower dog. Kiki got over their love affair in about four hours, but McDweebs took his vows seriously—"in sickness and in health" and all that…and clearly until the "death do they part" part.

How on earth did the Lylas get chosen to do this? Kiki wondered for the thousandth time. What had they done to deserve it?

Chapter 11

$\mathcal{P}$ ARKER WAS STANDING BY the only window in the dark video-edit studio watching Tribb and the rest of the Tigers stretch their hamstrings on the field. It was so sunny outside, so the opposite of this cramped, stuffy place. Tons of Wallys were already out on the bleachers. Where the Lylas belonged, she thought angrily. Weird James Hunter was walking around the production studio with his sweatshirt zipped up nearly to his chin and the bottom of his uniform shirt hanging out. He had his digital camera in his hands and he was bending down, lurking around corners with his lanky body and snapping photographs of who knows what. *The leg of a chair? The light switch? The gum stuck underneath a desk?* James got extra creeper points for having shaggy hair flopped down over his eyes and flipped up in all directions. It would have been cute if he'd styled it that way on purpose or if he was protesting the mistreatment of hairbrushes or something.

James's fingers moved quickly around the buttons of his camera like they knew exactly where they were going before they got there. For a moment Parker was transfixed by them.

He caught her staring.

Flustered, Parker shifted her eyes quickly to the clock above him, which, BTdubs, seemed to be ticking extra-slowly.

Kiki licked the tip of her finger and flipped though *Lucky* magazine. Ikea had her nose buried in her Latin book: "…*portō, portāre, portāvī, portātum,*" she practiced. Plum was lying in corpse pose on the floor next to Kiki with her pile of yellow slips balanced on top of her nose and her illegal striped undershirt untucked and pulled down past her uniform.

They were all supposed to be working, but what they were doing could officially be described as: Farting Around 101.

"They're saying this American Coquette bra makes you look a whole cup-size bigger." Kiki held up a page of her magazine to everybody.

Plum brushed the yellow slips off her face and looked at the model in the ad. She squished up her nose and turned her head sideways to get a better look at the image.

"I don't really think she needs to be a cup-size bigger." Ikea glanced up from her conjugations. "Her cups are already pretty big," she observed.

"My mom always says that they put these models in ads for age cream who are only, like, *twenty-five*," Kiki said. "So why would they need age cream if they're not that old…"

"I know," McDweebs chuckled (as he did in response to pretty much *anything* Kiki said). "That's so funny that they do that…" *Ha ha ha.* "They're always doing that."

"So…" Kiki continued as if McDweebs hadn't spoken at all (as she did in response to pretty much *anything* McDweebs said), "like why would this girl need to be any bigger?"

Plum looked so deeply into the photograph that she could've fallen in. Then she flopped back down on the floor and crossed her arms in front of her own washboard chest. "What do you do with all that…*flesh?*" she wondered aloud.

Parker peeked out the window to the field again. The Tigers

were already done stretching and had moved on to a scrimmage. *The world's out there. And I'm in here. What's wrong with this picture?*

"What are we doing here, you guys?" she finally blurted. She sat back on the windowsill and kicked the wall with the heel of her shoe. "I mean, *hello*. Reality check. Look at us!" Ikea took her nose out of her book. James stopped taking photographs of the ceiling. "We are *so* the last people in the world who should be doing this."

McDweebs looked disappointed—as if someone had just taken away his box of Raisinets before the movie even started.

"Except *you*, Leonard," Parker corrected. "You're actually the *perfect* person in the world who should be doing this."

"We should blow it off and go to the Orion store," Plum said from the floor. "I really want that new black glitter case for my phone."

"I could be home scooping up Snicker's poop-bombs," Kiki suggested, "or yanking out my hair, or having a heart-to-heart convo with Bunny…really *anything* would be more entertaining than *this*." Kiki nodded over to McDweebs. "Anything would be less torturous than sitting here watching IckDweebs-May obber-slay all over the omputer-cay."

For the first time in his life, he didn't smile at her. "I am not slobbering," McDweebs insisted. "I am carefully removing dust particles from the keyboard with a lint-free cloth, if you don't mind. *Iki-Kay.*"

Kiki scowled. "Whatevs."

Parker felt like the room had no air in it. She could be out there right now, she thought, watching Tribb, popping cinnamint Tic-Tacs, waiting until he finished playing soccer, until he ran up to her all sweaty-ish and asked her if she had any plans for Fall Sosh. Then she could go home, practice glamorous updos for the event, upload her photos from the Vineyard to FB, think through the details of the outfit to wear to the big game against Fox Chapel, and IM something cute to Tribb after the whole Fall-Sosh-invitation-moment at the field. Her palms began to get clammy.

She *didn't ask* to be a *Wallingford Academy Today* producer. She *didn't ask* to miss every populartunity that there was.

"I hate this room," Plum said.

"Maybe we should just sort of *forget* to do the webcast," Kiki suggested.

"Hotchkiss will have a nutter…" Plum said. "Worst case, we'll get detention."

Parker was going through the alternatives in her head.

"Robert Pattinson got expelled from school when he was twelve," Kiki announced with a glimmer.

"My grandmother is *so* sending me to Our Lady of Fatima no matter what I do." Plum held up her stack of slips. "So I really couldn't give a whup what happens."

Parker peeked outside again. Practice would be over soon. Her heart was pounding away. She had to tell them the truth about her home sitch before it was too late. They would understand why she couldn't do the webcast no matter what happened. She summoned the courage to spit it out. "*I…I…*"

"We *have* to do it."

The other voice came out of nowhere. It was quiet but powerful. Ikea shut her textbook and stood up from her chair.

"We *have* to do it." Ikea looked around the room. "…*I* have to do it, you guys," she said. "My dad is president of the board.

He'll kill me if I mess this up." She was breathing fast. Her gray-green eyes could have shot holes right through the walls. "I need this on my record," she said. "For Yale."

"But you're not going to Yale for *five* years, Ike," Kiki reminded her. (Kiki always said what everyone was secretly thinking.)

"*I* have to do this, you guys," Ikea repeated. She was as serious as Parker had ever seen her. "I can't bail."

Parker closed her eyes. She could feel the pain well up behind her eyelids. All her years had amounted to nothing. Her life was over. She actually felt it floating away like dandelion fluff shaken away from its stem.

If Ikea had to do it, then so did she—so did all of them. It was rule number one. The rule that was never changed, amended, reversed, or modified. *Friends first.*

The one rule that would never be broken.

Parker held her left hand up to Ikea's. Plum stood up and so did Kiki. Their four silver rings met in the center. Neither James nor McDweebs joined them but they stood too, perhaps sensing some sort of ritualistic activity. Parker suppressed a smile. Like it or not, they were all in this together.

"We're in," Parker bravely announced. The secret would just have to wait.

Chapter 12

*H*OW TO MAKE A nightmare mildly acceptable? Stick together.

Every afternoon, instead of going out to watch Tribb's practice or trying out updos for Fall Sosh or getting an airbrush tan just to boost things back to the way they were naturally, the producers of *Wallingford Academy Today* made their way down the hall, past the lower level of the Hunt Memorial Library, past the nurse's office, past the two old phone booths and the bomb shelter entrance and the row of Super-Screens…to the most comatastic room in the whole school: the *Wallingford Academy Today* studio.

Together they stayed until the nurse went home, until the Super-Screens darkened for the night, until Arthur the janitor was finished buffing the second floor…until life, as they knew it, ceased to exist. Together they stayed when they should have been home tending to their Facebook pages, maintaining their prime position on the populadder. But now that position was up for grabs.

Plum found the cans of beige and off-beige paint behind some computer boxes in the storage closet. She put together the set exactly like they had the year before. And the year before that. She stayed completely within the color palette, which was a major-domo accomplishment for a rebel like Plum. Worse,

Parker noted, Plum's overalls and hi-tops were splashed with beige paint. Chunks of white spackling paste streaked through her hair and spotted her perfectly made-up face. (Though she managed to make dirty work look like a fashion trend.)

It took four afternoons for Plum to get it to look exactly like it was in the archive.

Parker had to admit: she was impressed. In the end, the set looked pretty...*smart*. They all agreed. They tried to stay positive.

"'Perfect Passive Participles—the Key to Understanding Latin Conjugations.'" Ikea ran through a few of her supersmart ideas for segments with the rest of the Lylas.

"Passive Participles..." Kiki considered the baffling concept.

"Sweet," Plum said with a wave of her brown paintbrush. "Loving the Latin thing, Ike."

Ikea was the ideal Segments Producer. No one else understood a word of it—which meant Hotchkiss would love it. Not to mention the Yale admissions committee. They were making it happen. *That's* what really mattered.

"Which one do you think, Park?" Kiki had her hand covering the answer on the "Who Wore it Better" page in *Us* magazine. She pushed the pages across the table to Parker. "Eliza or Cameron?" she asked. "And it's so obvy you're definitely not going to get it wrong."

"Aren't you supposed to be practicing the lunch menu?" Parker asked her.

"I am *not* rapping the lunch menu," Kiki assured everyone in the whole world. "Like, hello!"

"Macaroni and Cheese, would you please..." McDweebs rapped enthusiastically from behind the Orion 2000. "Apple Cobbler, if you bother—"

"Thank you, Slim Shady."

"You do *not* have to rap the lunch menu, Keek." Parker pushed the *Us* back across the table. "But you have to do *something.*"

"Fine!" Kiki reluctantly shut her magazine and marched off to mope elsewhere.

As awful as all this was, Parker Bell was still Parker Bell and she was not going to leave behind something embarrassing for everyone to laugh at. Her face was not going to be projected up on the Super-Screen with people in the audience saying, "Who was she? Who remembers?" She was not going to be archived in an Orion kiosk forever as dork bait. Not after seven long years of doing everything right.

So while Parker was not fugly, and her forehead height-to-face-size ratio was not out of normal range (she measured), she took on the worst possible part of the assignment: the host of Snoozeville.

• • •

"Helloandwelcometo *WallingfordAcademyToday.*"

Parker practiced the welcome from her spot behind the brown teacher's desk and the sea-of-mud soundstage. The smell of Plum's fresh paint made her woozy.

Silently, the show's official cameraman, James, trained the video camera on her. He adjusted his lens with his quick and skillful hands as she sat there. Then he got down on one knee to get a different angle on the next take, then stood on a chair, then back down to his knee. It was like *America's Next Top Model*, minus the cool clothes, the $100,000 CoverGirl contract, and (*duh*viously) the next top model.

Parker felt strangely nervous as James moved around her—more nervous than when she had to recite Lady Macbeth's "Out, damn spot!" soliloquy for the whole Shakespeare class last year. It felt like a million sets of eyes were on her instead of just thirty-two.

James's face was blocked by the camera as he shot the video. All Parker saw were his long limbs and supersonic fingers as he circled around her like the headless horseman. He was also a lot taller than she'd realized.

"HelloandwelcometoTallingfordWacademyToday…" Parker repeated, only this time her heart was beating so fast she flubbed it up. *"Hallingford…Callingford…"* She tried again but she felt self-conscious being the center of all this attention—like she was the turkey in the middle of the table on Thanksgiving. Did her forehead look unusually large? Or shiny? Could James see something bad through his camera? Did something go wrong with her show?

"Hello and…*and…and…*" she tried again.

James stopped filming. He put the camera down at his side and pushed his free hand deep into his pocket. He looked off to the side like he was giving her privacy while she changed out of her bathing suit (which, as Parker imagined it, would have been a whole lot less embarrassing). She couldn't tell if he was mad at her for messing up the line, if he thought he could say the stupid thing any better, or if he was just waiting to leave. The whole thing made her very, very angry.

"Do you *only* know how to take pictures of the lunch ladies serving up macaroni and cheese?" Parker snapped.

James didn't answer her. His silence drove her bonkies.

Parker stood up from behind the teacher's desk. "Do you know how to use that camera, James, or what?" she demanded.

James looked directly at her. The camera wasn't in between them now but suddenly she was even more self-conscious without it. And James's eyes weren't dark at all, Parker realized. They were bright, arctic blue. They only looked dark because of the thick eyelashes that surrounded them. They were more puzzling than weird. They kicked the breath right out of her.

"I know how to use it," James replied.

The sudden sound of his voice was startling. It was the first thing he'd said to her since maypole. A rush of nerves came fluttering up from her stomach making her neck flush.

It took Parker a minute to calm down enough to try her line again.

James lifted the camera back up to his shoulder.

"Okay then." Parker cleared her throat. "Hello…and welcome to *Wallingford Academy Today*." At long last the words came out flawlessly. From behind the camera, Parker thought she caught the glimmer of a smile crossing James's face.

• • •

It took more than a week of prep-work, eight afternoons of filming (three entirely devoted to Kiki and her lunch menu), and a week more of McDweebs's editing, for the team to finish the webcast—in all, almost a whole month.

During the process, they consumed three family-sized bags of pretzel crisps from the Convenience Mart, a box of frosted brown sugar cinnamon Pop Tarts, four cans of Pringles: one sour cream and onion, one ranch-flavored, two original (McDweebs became Pringles's Facebook Friend), and countless packages of Mr. Churros. Kiki said she was committing carbocide as she stuffed another handful of Cap'n Crunch in her food cave. Ikea worried about their collective Carbo Footprint. Parker just wanted it all to be over. She wanted it to be tomorrow already. She wanted Matin to be over.

In what had sadly degenerated into a lonely ritual, Parker stole another glance through the single studio window toward the soccer field. Amazing: the days were already getting shorter, the sun already a little lower in the sky. She smiled when she saw Tribb. He was bouncing a ball up and down on his head and laughing. She imagined herself sitting down there on the bleachers. Her butt would be cold from the metal but it didn't matter—just being near Tribb would keep her warm. He would wave to her when he ran by, maybe give her the secret signal for something only the two of them knew about.

"We're loving the noof, right? She's super-sweet."

Plum's announcement interrupted Parker's mental moment with some serious annoyment. The words screeched through Parker's mind as clear as if someone had actually said them. *Cricket* was out there on the bleachers with a cold butt—not Parker. She was leaning back on one elbow with a leg dangling off the bleacher. She kept twirling her hair around in her fingers again and again and flipping her head back when she laughed.

Did someone say Obsessive Repulsive Disorder?

Courtney and Tinsley (Parker's fourth and fifth best friends, she had to remind herself) were one bleacher below. They clapped as Tribb took a corner kick. Parker's jaw tightened. Courtney had a suspiciously dark tan considering tennis camp had ended six weeks ago. No doubt she had fake-n-baked it. And Tinsley's hair was looking a little too bumpiterrific. *How many of those things did she have in there?*

Parker turned away and caught her reflection on one of the many Orion monitors. Her tan was now gone. Her barely there highlights were *hardly* there. Her new cashmere sweater had spent up all of its precious new-time doing things that didn't count for anything. And her Carbo Footprint had become unbelievably large.

A whole month of afternoons completely wasted…and it showed.

Outside, Tinsley brought two fingers to her mouth and whistled. Cricket jumped up and down. Apparently Tribb had scored. Or something. But Parker couldn't hear any of it. Just the irritating noise of James putting away the video camera, the soft rustle of Kiki opening her third Pop Tart of the day, Ikea turning the pages of Jansen's *History of Art*, Plum lacing her hi-tops back on her feet, and the buzz and ping of McDweebs copying the final webisode onto a DVD to slip under Hotchkiss's door.

There was no denying it. She was completely off Tribb's radar.

• • •

"Balsamic or lemon vinaigrette tonight?"

Ellen Bell stood next to the sink at the center island of the kitchen and ripped open a bag of chopped lettuce, then tossed it in the salad spinner and added water from the sink. She was still wearing her suit and coat and her purse was still flung over her shoulder. In a frenzy, she rushed around the kitchen, pulling things out of the refrigerator and sticking them in the microwave. Parker chopped carrots on the cutting board across from her.

"I don't care," Parker muttered as she chopped.

"Crumbled bleu cheese?" Ellen wiped her hands on a kitchen towel and finally took off her coat. "Oh my goodness, my bag!"

"Bleu Cheese is fine if that's what you want," Parker said. She was barely conscious of uttering the words. They seemed to come from a machine inside her. A cold, unfeeling Orion computer.

Ellen stopped what she was doing and stared at Parker. "You hate bleu cheese."

"Then why did you ask me?" Parker groaned.

"What is the matter with you, Parker?" Ellen demanded with a frown.

Only everything. Parker felt like her insides were whirling around faster and faster. Soon her head would simply pop off. She tried to calm herself before she said anything stupid. *I am Parker Bell. I am confident, cool, and on top of things.*

"Look," Ellen began. "I am trying *very hard* to get work that will pay me as much as I was making from Siddie's job so that we can stay here..." She pointed to her purse and coat, now draped across the other end of the kitchen island. She tried to smile, but her lower lip quivered. "And it is not easy, sweetheart, when all you've done for ten years is baby-sit a rock star." Her voice cracked. Parker really didn't want her mother to start to cry. "And if your life is so miserable that you can't appreciate that..." She composed herself and then some. "Then we really should just move right now," she said sensibly. "Fox Chapel has a great school system and I'm sure you'd make lots of new friends. And you wouldn't be that far away from your old friends."

The calm tone of her mother's voice frightened her. She wasn't just *thinking* about moving. She'd gone into planning mode. Parker knew she had to think quickly.

"I'm just stressed about biology," Parker said with her I'm-just-stressed-about-school face. "Kiki's my lab partner, so you know what that means," she said casually. "Winkle hates me... and I got a little behind in my reading..." She listed truths. Truth always made lies more believable.

Ellen relaxed a little. She took a bottle of salad dressing out of the refrigerator.

"Everything will work out fine, Mom," Parker assured her.

"Did you have to dissect the baby shark yet?" Ellen asked with a laugh.

"That's next week's torture."

"And that's it?" Ellen asked suspiciously. "Everything else is going well?"

"Everything else..." Parker gathered up the slices of carrot and dumped them into the bowl with the lettuce, "is perfect."

Chapter 13

*P*ER PROTOCOL, PARKER, KIKI, Ikea, and Plum met beside the old phone booths in Freeman Auditorium before Matin for Hair & Makeup and mints. They watched as Wallys funneled past them in the foyer toward the doors. Most everyone followed the Lylas's lead and did a discreet check of hair, a fresh application of Lipglass, and a handful of some minty candy before Matin. Also per protocol, the boys always came in wearing enough Axe deodorant to make the whole auditorium smell like Dark Temptation and Impulse.

Hotchkiss had made a way bigger deal out of the day than any of them realized she would. Every Orion Super-Screen in the building rippled with giant 3-D graphics of the school seal. Just the sight of all that Latin waving on every wall of the school made Parker nervous enough to gobble up the entire pack of Tic-Tacs.

"*Semper Veritas,*" Plum repeated the motto at the bottom of the school seal. "What does that even *mean?*" she asked with a pop of her gum. "Stay *true?* To what?"

"Mottoes aren't supposed to mean anything, are they?" Parker said as she took out her Lipglass and reapplied. She watched as Emily Townsend copied her reapply move. "I thought they just stuck one on there because every school has one," she added.

"A good motto is supposed to be an expression of the guiding principal, spirit, or purpose of an organization." Ikea explained. "Something that everyone tries to be."

Kiki checked her reflection on the back of her phone. Nearly everybody who walked by checked her out, too. "Stay *pretty*," she said with a fluff of her hair. "Now *that's* a motto." She smiled. Parker almost laughed. Good old Keeks: she had the right idea.

Ikea stood on her tippy-toes and looked over the heads of students filtering in. She opened a second pack of Tic-Tacs and gobbled some up herself.

"You looking for your dad?" Parker asked, her mouth spicy with cinnamon flavoring.

Ikea shrugged. "I guess not really." She scanned the foyer once more. "He's pretty busy."

Kiki pulled the two sides of her cardigan tightly around her stomach as gobs of Wallys walked by. She'd been yanking on her sweater all morning, trying to cover up the results of two weeks of Pop Tarts.

"So you gained, like, three ounces, Keek." Plum took a few of Ikea's mints and chewed them up into her gum. "Big whup."

"You don't get it, Plum," Kiki protested. "This was supposed to be my super-skinny-jeans year."

Parker bit her thumbnail. She couldn't deal with the piddly Lylas tension right now. James looked over at her from his spot in the projection room. He was waiting for Hotchkiss to hand him the key drive that they'd made the night before. She was reminded again how she'd been wrong about James's eyes. They definitely weren't dark. They were like computer screen blue, lit from behind. There was something about them that made you want to keep looking—a page-turning mystery you'd better put down. Parker took her own advice and turned away.

Kenneth Accolola walked up to Kiki and gave her a backhand snap. "Hey?" He looked down at her stretched out sweater. "Wasn't this going to be our super-skinny-jeans year, Keeks? I thought we weren't eating." Kiki didn't return Kenneth's snap. "I've spent the entire week carbo-loading and repeating the phrase 'tofu corn dogs and chocolate turtle pie' like a thousand times. Okay, Kenneth?"

"No probs, Miss Pissy." Kenneth dismissed Kiki with a wave of his hand and swaggered into the auditorium. Parker would have reminded Kiki about the be-nice-to-Kenneth-you're-his-only-friend rule, but Kiki was too upset about the skinny-jeans year for Parker to get into it.

The Lylas followed a few yards behind Kenneth toward their row in the back of the eighth grade section.

Parker's jaw dropped.

Cricket Von Wielding was occupying a seat in the Premiums. So was Courtney Wallace.

Plum's gasp was audible. She nearly lost her gum. Even Ikea looked like she might have a hairy nip fit.

"*These…*" Kiki marched right up to them with a hand on her hip. "Are *our* seats." She looked right at Courtney (who last year had completely stolen Kiki's signature Flamenco-inspired approach to formal wear, which Kiki considered trademark infringement and further proof of Courtney's lack of the qualities necessary to become a Lyla).

Parker had to steady herself. This was a test. Of course it was. One of many. If she wanted to make the best of what she had left, she'd have to give up some things. Important things. *Look at Joan of Arc!*

"It's fine." Parker put her arm around Kiki's waist and poked a finger in her side. (Secret Signal: *Shut up!*) "It's totally, absolutely, completely fine for you guys to sit here," she said, "in *our* seats." She smiled, anger bubbling inside her. "The ones everybody knows belong to us."

Cricket looked up from Parker's seat with sharp eyes, her overly natural eyebrows and her matchie-matchie headband-tote thing, but said nothing.

"And Courtney," Parker continued sweetly, "It's really super-nice of you to show Cricket around this...*new* place." She took a deep breath and led the Lylas to the next best seats, the ones *next* to Cricket and Courtney. It would all be just fine.

Kiki grumbled as they pushed past Courtney and Cricket toward the places next to them. Parker tried to feel good (or at least *look* good) about it even though whisperings among the lower-on-the-populadder Wallys had clearly started. Yup, the news was going viral: the Lylas had given up their primo seats just so Miss Preptobismol and her trademark infringing BFF could sit in them.

"Aren't you *sooo* psyched, Parker?!?"

Parker practically jumped when Tinsley nudged in behind her and took the seat beside Courtney before any of them could sit down.

"Yeah," Parker said, taking the seat next to Tinsley. "Way psyched." Even though she couldn't see them, she could feel the eyes of Kiki, Ikea, and Plum on her as they sat down directly behind Cricket Von Full-of-Herself and the two Hangers-On. "And aren't you *sooo* psyched about the Big Game this weekend?" Tinsley added. "I've *so* been shopping all week for it. Go Tigers!!"

"The Big Game!" Parker exclaimed without even a hint of confusion. She'd been working so hard on the show that she'd completely forgotten it was this weekend. But how could she have forgotten? The Big Game was an immense event. And hopefully not her last. "*Totally* psyched..." Parker realized there was less than twenty-four hours to compose, collect, and beautify. This would be her first-kiss-with-Tribb day, after all. She'd have to set her alarm for super-early. "*So* shopped till I dropped," she added.

"It's one of the truly major-domo social opportunities of the year," Tinsley reminded Parker unnecessarily. "But I don't need to tell *you* that."

Parker tuned her out and scanned the rows up front for Tribb and the rest of the team. Kirby was trying to make it seem like he was just playing drums on the back of the seat next to him but really he was sort of staring in Plum's general direction, bobbing his head up and down and left and right to an imaginary song. Parker grimaced. *Maybe he has an actual medical problem?*

"He's here!" Ikea turned around. She yanked so hard on Parker's sleeve that she nearly popped a button. She shot up from her seat and waved. "Dad!" She tried to get his attention before she sat back down.

"That's great, Ike!" Parker fixed a stray bit of Ikea's glossy straight hair. She knew how important this was to Ikea, how living up to her dad's expectations probably wasn't all that easy. She was glad the Lylas had all stuck together.

Ikea turned toward Parker. "Thanks for doing this," she whispered. "I mean it. It means a lot to me."

"No probs." Parker smiled.

The lights dimmed, the audience quieted, and a spotlight lit the center of the stage. Death Breath was still looking around for one final victim before Matin began. Kiki quickly thrust a scrap of paper under Plum's chin. "Gum, hotshot," she said before the teacher could catch it.

"Thanks." Plum spit.

And the room went completely dark.

Chapter 14

$\mathcal{M}$ RS. ROUSE RAISED AND lowered her fingers on the piano keys one last time before Hotchkiss took her place behind the podium. There was a full minute of silence (not even a belch from Graham Henry) before the headmistress looked up into the spotlight and spoke. Allegra Oliphant made the mistake of clapping at that moment—it was a little like applauding in church.

"This year," Hotchkiss said with one of her evil Terminator smiles, "brings forth a time of change…" She pressed a button on her black Orion Tablet with the Genius Pen and the Super-Screens were suddenly filled with a collection of old, tea-stained images of Wallingford's first headmistress, Miss Thistle, and ancient pictures of Wallys—back when it was just a girls' school, when *Wallingford Academy Today* was just a stinky one-page newspaper. "It is a time of technological advancements beyond Miss Thistle's wildest imagination…And we here at Wallingford are on the *cutting edge*" (yes, she made the words sound super-scary) "of this brave new world." She used her stylus again and the surrounding screens switched from the ancient Wally images to the modern Orion Computers logo swirling around the room. "And again…" Hotchkiss kept it going at a clip. "I'd like to thank our generous Alumnae body for making these opportunities available to our students…"

Hello. Everyone got who she meant: Fitz Orion. If it weren't for him, *Wallingford Academy Today* would still just be a one-page newspaper.

"*Opportunities…*" Hotchkiss continued, "like our very own *Wallingford Academy Today* webcast."

Parker's heart began beating loudly in her chest. She tried to focus on posi-thoughts: laying out her outfit for the game tomorrow, taking a couple of "Coke or Pepsi?" quizzes with Plum, IMing it up with Tribb—being clever but not too LOL, sweet but not too emoticon overloaded, girlfriend-like but without ever coming out and exactly saying it that way.

Hotchkiss nodded to James in the back of the auditorium and held the stylus up at attention.

"And I hope you will enjoy the following," Hotchkiss said, "It is an…*an…*" She squinted up at the chandelier like she might find the right word up there. "An…*abecedarian* effort by our new and exceedingly talented team."

"Abecedarian?" Parker spun to Ikea. "That's good, right?"

Ikea looked perplexed. "I have no idea," she said.

If the word was too smart for Ikea, it probably meant it was pretty good. But good in Hotchkiss's eyes? That meant bad in every other way.

"We do look forward to the future efforts of our new staff." Hotchkiss looked directly at Parker. "And finally," she added quickly, "we wish Captain Tribble Reese and the Tigers the best of luck as they play the Fox Chapel Acorns at home to-morrow. Go Wallingford Tigers!" She pointed her wand at James and gave the signal to begin.

The room erupted in the excited hoots and hollers for the Tigers. Parker could hear Tribb and the team yelling in the front. Tinsley screeched out one of her mind-numbing whistles. It was so noisy just about everybody missed the entire first minute of the webisode—the host's introduction.

But Parker didn't miss it. Not a millisecond.

"Hello and welcome to *Wallingford Academy Today!*"

There she was. On the most humongous Orion Super-Screen in the building. Parker's nose alone was the size of the Statue of Liberty. That minute, *that minute of noise,* lasted about a hundred years.

Watching herself on the screen wasn't anything like watching herself in the mirror rehearsing her Academy Award acceptance speech or practicing "Hey, Tribb" poses. Every little part of her showed, the ugly parts especially: her crooked smile, the big freckle beside her eye, the baby fat still filling her cheeks, her egg-shaped head. Even the sound of her voice was horrible. Nasal, like she was honking instead of speaking.

But it wasn't her face or her voice that made Parker want to die right there; it was what showed underneath all that—the part of herself that she always thought she was hiding. The secret things she felt inside that no one, not even the Lylas, knew. Everything she felt was right there for everyone to see: stupid, insecure, afraid, lonely, uncomfortable, different. She looked like a part of her was missing. A big part. How could someone like that think she was something special? *How could anyone think I'm something special?*

Suddenly petrified, she looked back at James. Is this what he saw in his camera?

Parker barely heard a word of the next eleven minutes and fifty-three seconds. Instead of wanting it to be over, she never wanted it to end. She wanted to sit in the dark forever. *This isn't perfect one bit. This is the opposite of that.* She dreaded the lights coming up…

Plum's set looked great though. And Ikea's segment, "Milestone Cases in Supreme Court History," was Yale-worthy. Parker squinted across the sea of Wallys at Ikea's father. The back of his head didn't reveal much, but he had to have been impressed.

"We're loving the webcast, Park!" Courtney leaned in and whispered.

"Awesomage!" Tinsley added.

"Way better than Allegra Elephant could have done!"

"Way."

"…And the vegetarian selection of tofu corn dogs is followed by your choice of chocolate turtle pie or butterscotch pudding…"

"Maybe my other side was my better side after all?" Kiki critiqued her performance.

"This is *definitely* the best of all your sides," Plum assured her. After fifteen hours of filming and hundreds of takes in every possible direction, they were all experts on which side was Kiki's best. And this was definitely *not* it—Plum was just sick of discussing it.

"You think I look okay? I mean, not the most disgusting mammal on the plant, right?" Kiki asked. "How can anyone expect to look good in a uniform anyway?"

"You look fine, Kiki. Great." Parker tried to calm her. "Very…British. Okay?"

Kiki seemed to take Parker's word for it. She smiled as she watched the rest of the webcast play out.

Chapter 15

$\mathcal{A}$ FTERWARD, WALLYS SWARMED ON the Lylas in the Freeman Auditorium foyer and told them how much they liked the show. It was kind of like a rule that everyone in the school followed even though it wasn't written down or anything. People had to say nice things to you like they actually meant it. Sometimes they even said super-nice things and made you feel like they actually meant it. But Parker knew when congratulations meant nothing. She'd been guilty of saying them herself.

"Cute!"

"Sweet!"

"Fantastilistic!"

"K-L!"

"G-Z!"

"I loved all the intellectual junk!"

"Way better than Allegra!"

Duncan Middlestat gave them all a double-thumbs up. "Abecedarian!" he said.

Whatever that meant.

"Keeks!" McDweebs came up to Kiki and tried to do a fist-bump with her.

Kiki put both hands on her hips. "Okay, here's the thing, McDweebs…" she explained. "Kiki Allen does not do high-fives, low-fives, peace-outs, man-shakes, skin-its, and definitely, for sure, beyond a shadow of a doubt, bro-bumps."

McDweebs took careful note of her directions and made sure she was completely finished with her list before he said anything. "But other than that, I can say hello?" he asked hopefully.

"Yeah. Sure." Kiki rolled her eyes at Parker. It was the I-wish-things-were-back-to-normal look. "Why would I give a rat what you do?"

McDweebs did the hi-to-low-chain-yank, usually reserved for soccer players who just scored a goal. "Epic," he chirped as he walked off to class.

The bell was about to ring, and Parker stayed put, watching as Ikea finally saw her father in the corner of the foyer talking on his phone—in his pinstripe suit, power tie, and flashing Bluetooth headset. His deep, forceful voice filled the two-story space. Ikea ran right up to him.

"Dad!"

He held a hand up to her as he spoke. "We won't accept, Jim…" he said sternly into his mouthpiece. He sounded like a bulldozer on the phone. "If Standish wants to obfuscate the issues with some *antediluvian* argument, he better know who he's dealing with because they *will* fail with that misjoinder—"

"Did you see my segment on milestone Supreme Court rulings, Dad?" Ikea pressed. Her smile was on all 500 Watts.

He put his fingers on the receiver. "*I'm on a call, sweetheart,*" he mouthed. "…What part of 'we won't accept' don't you understand, Jim?" he continued.

Parker winced. Ikea stood there waiting patiently for her father to finish his call even though the bell had rung and the foyer was nearly empty. Parker saw Ikea catch herself doing the Birdie then folded her arms tightly in front of her for safekeeping.

"*Hutchinson v. Proxmire* spells it out clear as day…" Mr. Bentley put his fingers over the receiver again. *"A for effort, Ikea."* He patted his daughter on the shoulder. *"Very decent,"* he said before he went back to his call. "An offer like that means nothing to me, Jim. It's just one less Picasso hanging on my wall."

Ikea's smile melted from the enormous lightbulb into one of those squiggly lines they draw onto cartoon-people's faces when they're sick.

Mr. Bentley was still on his call when he left through the side entrance. He waved once more to his daughter before the door closed behind him.

Parker waited as Ikea stood there silently in the Freeman Foyer. She was ten minutes late for class.

Chapter 16

The six rules of the Big Game:

1. No Snuggies. No Slankets. Not even cashmere. And absolutely no headbands.
2. Be nice to Kenneth (u know who u are). You're his only friend.
3. Totes are still in.
4. Cherry Carmex before kissing. Dot dot dot.
5. Mingle with the less popular—work the bleachers.
6. No stiletto heels (u still know who u are).

THE NIGHT BEFORE THE big game, Parker posted the Rules in the private section of her profile. Making up rules always got her back in a posimood. Rules were like happy pre-lated birthday presents—there was nothing bad about them.

It was already late, but Parker wasn't even near-sleepy. She was too excited about her first kiss with Tribb. In spite of everything that had happened, it was destiny.

She hadn't been on Facebook in ages and there were so many things to do. She kicked off her furry slippers, tucked her feet up under her on the Darcy chair, and made herself comfortable for the long haul.

"You want?" Ellen opened Parker's door with a pint of Double Chocolate Chunk in her hand and an extra spoon. She showed her daughter a glimpse of the dark, gooey contents.

Parker had been avoiding her mother, or more specifically, avoiding any bad news her mother might have to deliver. There were no new clients, no big sale of furniture on eBay, and Ellen hadn't put on a business suit in weeks.

"No thanks." Parker attached the cable to her camera and began uploading an album she titled "Summer." She was determined not to get distracted from her mission, not even for Double Chunk.

"It's starting to get cold out, don't you think?" Ellen asked.

Parker was suspicious of the question and didn't want to answer. Besides, it was kind of rhetorical. *Of course it was getting cold out. That's what "fall" does.*

"I need you to keep your room straightened up," Ellen said. "The real estate brokers could need to get in here without much warning."

"Okay." Parker poured all of her attention on Facebook, but she still heard every word her mother was saying. She watched as her photos appeared on her screen. The whole summer flashed by quickly: lobster rolls at Larsen's in Menemsha, making faces on the beach with Andy Raskin (just friends, JSYK), Kiki showing off her "favorite, new" (now "icky, old") sunglasses before her trip to London.

"The house won't sell right away," Ellen said. "It might not be everybody's cup of tea, right?"

The nicest mansion on one of the nicest streets in neighborhood? Completely renovated by a neurotically neat architect? "Right," Parker mumbled.

"How's school going for you?"

"Good." Parker looked up and smiled. "Really good."

"Don't stay up too late," Ellen said with a spoon of Double Chunk in her mouth.

"K."

"And I'm really glad school's going so well," Ellen said before she closed Parker's door behind her.

"Me too."

"G'night."

"G'night."

Parker stared at her work. She now had twenty-six albums in all on her profile, including photos from every year of her life. The albums said everything you needed to know about Parker Bell. Not bad…

Maybe Facebook is my actual home? Wherever you go, there it is. Facebook Friends stay with you.

• • •

What R u wearing for game? : - ?

A text from Kiki came up on her phone.

No clue. U?

DGT!! n0thing in closet! >: [Urrgh!!

You'll find sumthng. (-.-) <zzz>

Me2. <zzz> L8r. LYLAS

LYLAS 2 ;)

Parker shut the phone and went back to her profile. She was almost afraid to open her Friend requests—she'd gone the whole two weeks without checking in. A serious Facebook felony for which she would be surely punished. She hated when she got this backblogged. Nervously she clicked it open.

You have 4 friend requests.

Exqueeze me? Four? Just four?

She had to close Facebook and open it again to be sure it was right. She shut down her computer and rebooted. She looked to make sure all the cable thingies were in the right socket thingies. She even tried to write the Facebook help desk, but that only sent her to a FAQs page. But no matter how many times she turned things off and on, the words were still the same. Four requests? In two weeks? She usually got that in an hour.

She opened the requests page.

There was still the one request from Ellen Bell. (Still? Really? Couldn't she take the hint?) Then there was one from McDweebs, one from a girl who lived in a place called Christmas Island, and one from Pringles.

She stared at the Friends, or more specifically, the lack of Friends, but it just did not compute. She was Parker Bell. She paid attention to these things. She continuously updated and polished. She'd even told Cricket Von Steal-a-Seat she'd definitely confirm her if she Friended.

So where were all her new Friends?

Reluctantly she accepted McDweebs. (It sort of felt like he deserved the cred after pouring through all those outtakes of Kiki and her best sides.) She accepted the girl from Christmas

Island on GPs. (A person who lived on an island called Christmas might give her profile a festive edge.) She deleted Pringles. (Because no one with any self-respect should have potato chips as a Friend.) And she left her mother in limbo. (Obvs.)

It was almost midnight when she clicked on Tinsley Reardon's profile.

Tinsley still had under three-hundred Friends. But she'd added this cool new app that animated her main profile pic— She was waving over and over again in the simple but realistic, looped video-slash-photograph. Even though her Bumpit barely moved, the pic was fully animated.

Parker had never seen any app like it before.

Frantic, she clicked on another Friend, and another, and another. They all had the new app. Laurel had a goldfish swimming around in a bowl. Natalie blew kisses. Tribb held up his Tiger's team shirt and gave the rock-on sign with his hand again. Samantha. Emily. Jason. Beaver. Even Pringles had it. The only Friends whose faces were frozen in one spot were Kiki, Ikea, and Plum. None of them moved anything anywhere. They looked like mere Muggles by comparison.

It was 1:00 a.m. when Ellen Bell cracked the door open again.

"Parker?! Why aren't you in bed?" But Parker was still combing through the new apps pages, trying desperately to find the program that pretty much everyone else on the planet now had.

"In a sec…" she said. "Just one more thing…" Nearly deranged, she scrolled through another page. "I need this one thing…this one little thing…" She sounded like a psycho. Even *she* knew that.

"Go to bed, Parker." Ellen shut off the lights. "Now."

E.O.D. = End of Discussion.

Parker had to accept the fact that she wasn't going to find the app tonight. She was tired and cross-eyed. Not to mention un-updated and unpolished. Worst of all, she hadn't even picked out her first-kiss-with-Tribb outfit. After her mom shut the door, she sat on the edge of her bed and placed the laptop on the table beside her. There was just one more thing she had to do. She went to her home page.

Parker stared hard into the blank status box.

Parker is...

The cursor blinked hypnotically. She nearly fell asleep watching it. Her mind was weak but she still found the words tumbling around like Tic-Tacs in her head.

Parker is...crossing her fingers. Go Tigers!

She shut the laptop and crawled under the covers. *Worst. Status. Update. Ever...*

Chapter 17

*Y*ou up?" Kiki asked as soon as Parker picked up the phone.

It was Saturday morning, 7:30 a.m. On the nose. Only six hours until the Big Game. The Lylas had to get ready.

"U*rgsh*rg," Parker replied in the only way she could after just six hours of sleep.

"Tell me about it." Kiki agreed.

Plum's cell phone rang a minute later. "You up?" Parker asked.

"*Nico, you air biscuit! Gimme back my stupid undershirt, toolhead!*" Plum answered. "I'm up."

Ikea's cell phone rang a minute later. "You up?" Plum asked.

"I'm eating breakfast." Ikea crunched. "Grape Nuts!"

Their watches were synchronized. Their phones were charged. They would meet on the north side of the big tree in front of the stairs in exactly five hours and forty-five minutes. They reviewed the Rules and wished each other luck.

• • •

Kiki sat on the pink satin chair in her five-hundred-square-foot, climate-controlled closet. She ate a bowl of Fruit Loops while she contemplated her outfit. Both crystal chandeliers had been turned on as well as the gallery lights that lit the many rows of shoes and dresses from above and the ones that illuminated the glass shelves from below. The inlaid gold stars in the marble floor sparkled in the light.

She pulled a Diavolo blouse out from the Diavolo section of the closet and hung it up on one of the gold hooks on the far wall. She took another spoonful of cereal. That's when the freak-out began. Her flat head low riders (the perfect jeans for the blouse) were at the cleaners.

Placing her cereal on the floor, Kiki bolted out of the closet to tell Esmerelda, the second floor housekeeper, to call the dry cleaners and demand they put a rush on the jeans.

The jeans, according to the cleaners, according to Esmerelda, couldn't be ready in time.

The freaking out persisted.

It took the next four hours to even semi-sort out the outfit sitch. By the time it was over, thirty-four blouses had been detonated like bombs all over the marble floor.

On the other hand, the finished outfit was even better than she'd imagined. It was her own personal brand of spectacularity. A ledge in the making.

"Yes," she said when she looked in the mirror. "Distressingly good."

• • •

"I saw an ad..." Plum told the saleswoman at American Coquette. "In a magazine..."

"The Fantasia!" The saleswoman exclaimed. "The Fantasia is our bestseller," she confided more quietly.

The saleswoman led Plum to a dressing room in the back and laid a dozen styles of bras across a gilded chair in the corner of the room. Plum had no clue how long it took to try on bras but it seemed to take far longer than she imagined. There were clips and straps and crisscross thingies and they all needed to be adjusted, tightened and clipped. All behind a locked and barricaded dressing room door, of course. There was turning to the side wearing a bra, singing into a hairbrush wearing a bra, standing on tippy-toes wearing a bra, putting on Lipglass wearing a bra, and pretending to talk to Kirby Vanderbilt in the mirror. You know, just saying "Hey, Kirby. Yeah, I know. Totally. Me too."

All while *wearing a bra!!*

• • •

Ikea sat on the edge of her tub and waited for the hot comb to heat up. She divided her hair into tiny sections and applied Seal N' Shine to the ends. She started with the pieces in the back at her neckline and clipped the other sections out of the way. She glided the hot comb down each small, course segment in turn.

That was the key—only doing a little bit at a time. She had to reheat the comb a bunch of times and apply a few more coats of Seal N' Shine before all of her hair was done. She finished by pressing down at the top on either side of her part as flat as it would go.

When she was done, her hair was as soft and silky as any other Wally's. You couldn't really tell what it was like when it was natural. Even *she* didn't remember.

She squeezed solution onto each of her contact lenses and looked in the mirror at her dark, brown eyes. It only took a moment before they turned back to normal again. First the left, then the right. Colorfresh Pure Hazel. As clear and cool as the sea. Her signature color.

She remembered the quote that she and Divya had liked so much. She could almost hear the words being spoken. They felt like a warm blanket being wrapped around her. She looked up at her bulletin board on the wall beside her desk and at the photographs of some of the inspiring people she'd tacked to the board.

In her mind, the picture of Mahatma Gandhi began to move. He sat on the ground like a yogi with a white sheet draped around him and reached his hand out toward Ikea. "Be the change, Ikea," Gandhi said. He even pronounced her name correctly—like the lodge, not the store.

Martin Luther King agreed. He held his fist high above his microphone. "Be the change," he yelled to the crowd and then turned to Ikea and nodded.

Now it was Tyra Banks's turn—looking fierce in her red dress with her hand on her hip.

"Be the change, Ike," Tyra concurred with a gleaming smile.

• • •

"Capital O, capital M, capital G!" Ikea gasped. "You. Look. *Good!*"

Parker *did* look good, yes. But not in a conceited, she-thought-she-was-so-great kind of way. More like in a positive-self-image kind of way. (Seriously big diff.)

The weeks in the production studio had actually helped focus her energy on the morning. The first outfit she picked out (chunky beige cashmere sweater, vintage leather belt, soft, worn-in, super-approachable jeans, a minor touch of bling) worked. No makeup look—flawless. Tanning lotion—not an orange streak anywhere. She didn't even have to do her hair twice. The first blow-dry came out just right.

It was the perfect first-kiss outfit. A very touchable look.

Or maybe it was *too* touchable, she worried…a look de-signed for close-up flirtation only. *Would it work just as well*

110

from far away? If she didn't catch Tribb's attention in the first place, there'd be no first kiss. No need for the fuzzy sweater and approachable jeans. Maybe she should have worn something brighter to flag him down (in a perfectly subtle way)? Or maybe it wasn't about the outfit at all. Maybe it was about action. Big gestures. A little drama. And she wondered if her breath smelled good. If his breath smelled good. If he'd want a big wedding—like a Plaza blow-out with all their friends. Or would he rather save the money and do something small. In a wine cave in France maybe. Something completely gorgeous and candlelit. A night everyone would remember. Maybe she should have worn her other jeans.

For an uncomplicated species, boys made things way too complicated.

"Thanks, Ike," Parker said. "You. Look. *More* good!"

Birdies all around.

It was impossible not to notice Plum as she sauntered up to their meeting spot, the big tree near the stairs. She had on a new pair of black Converse that zipped up to her knees like boots. Her short, hot pink kilt matched the streak in her hair. Her zip-up hoodie was tiny and tight.

Plum was glowing! Plum was beautiful! Plum had *breasts*!?

"Wow." Parker and Ikea said at the same time.

Neither mentioned the new addition to Plum's front yard. They just smiled and nodded.

"Nice...*shirt* and stuff," Parker said.

"Your *hair* looks fantabulous!" Ikea added.

"Yeah..." Plum tucked a shock of hair behind her ear. "I used some new product."

"I'll say!" Kiki sashayed up to them in shiny, black,

over-the-knee boots and skinny, raw selvage jeans made by a company so exclusive and undiscovered that nobody but the Super-Futures had ever heard of it. The broad collar of her red tunic was up over her head like a hood, and mirror-black sunglasses covered half of her face. She was pretending like her outfit was no big deal when everyone knew perfectly well that she'd just turned her zillion-square-foot closet inside out for that look. (Kiki would turn her closet inside out just to find the right pair of pajamas.) "Nice *boobs*, Plum," Kiki added bluntly.

"Thanks." Plum crossed her arms in front of her chest. "Yours are *way* nicer," she teased. "Way."

Parker chewed a handful of Ikea's Tic-Tacs and reapplied her Lipglass. She could already hear the Wallingford Academy marching band going through the old favs. Warm-up would be over and the Big Game would be starting soon.

"*Noblesse oblige*," Parker reminded the Lylas as they turned in unison and marched toward the bleachers via the shortest and most nervy route: straight through the soccer field. Kiki had to walk on the balls of her feet so that the stiletto heels of her boots wouldn't sink into the muddy field.

Hate to say I told her so, but...

"The rules are there for a reason, Keek," Parker said.

They both looked down at her half-sunk shoes.

The autumn sun was warm but the air was chilly enough to merit a sweater. In other words, it was the perfect weather to be someone's girlfriend.

Parker picked up a handful of colorful leaves from a pile on the ground and tossed them into the air above her head. (And it wasn't just because she knew that kind of thing would look really cute if Tribb was watching her…which he *definitely* was…and that from far away your gestures had to be big to be noticed…she actually liked the way the autumn leaves smelled when they were tossed up into the air. She couldn't help it if some people, aka Tribb, noticed it.)

Kenneth Accolola saved the highest visibility spot on the bleachers for Kiki and the rest of the Lylas. "Are you still all miffed at me about the carb-binge incident, Keeks?"

"Moi? Miffed?" Kiki slid in next to Kenneth and linked her arm through his. "Of course not, darls."

"Because I'm dying over those boots! They are totally ferosh," Kenneth admired. "Your closet must be a mess."

Kiki giggled. "Esmerelda and I aren't speaking."

The rest of the Lylas slid in beside Kiki and Kenneth. *The Bleacher Spot: top row, center, shoes resting on second-to-top row. Nothing but blue sky behind their heads.*

Parker surveyed the field and saw Tribb kicking the ball around with Beaver and Kirby. Tribb never looked better than he did in his soccer uniform, she thought. Parker reached into her pocket to make sure the tube of Carmex was there.

Cherry Carmex before kissing. Dot, dot, dot. Check.

She'd passed the test. After a month of being holed up in that horrible studio, Tribb would see her and realize his destiny as the perfect EGB for Parker Bell. And she would know— she made the EGB Dream List in sixth, refined it in seventh, tweaked it at the beach…and then there he was all along: Tribb. The list in human form.

- Dimple
- Fair-to-tall height

113

- Not fat. But not a twig
- Tiny imperfection: nose or crooked tooth
- Tans easily
- Uses fork correctly
- Nice ears and hands
- Athletic but nothing dangerous
- Has friends
- No fart jokes
- Doesn't blow-dry
- Doesn't judge others
- Likes me for me
- Smells like Outdoor Fresh fabric softener sheets

She tried not to let herself get too excited about Fall Social but she couldn't help it. For everyone else it was the first black tie event of the school year and certainly the most important social event before Christmas, but given the way things were going at home, it would probably be Parker's last event ever. It was her last chance to be who she was...

Kirby stopped warming up and turned when he saw Plum climb into her seat. The soccer ball whacked him in the face.

"Smooth move." Plum rolled her eyes.

"Hey!" Tribb called up from the field. He held both hands up in the same rock-on gesture he had on his profile.

He'd noticed the autumn leaves toss!

Parker stood up in the bleachers and yelled back to him. "Go Tigers!" She was excited to have a better reply to "Hey" than "Hey." *Score one: Parker—*

"Hey!" A voice echoed from the bleachers below.

It was Cricket in the first row waving in Tribb's direction, her macramé bracelet flopping around. Her blond hair looked like tinsel in the sun.

Parker's eyes narrowed. She squinted at Tribb and tried to determine exactly where his rock-on fingers were pointed—at Parker's bleacher? Or at the governor's daughter? But the whistle blew before she could get an exact coordinate on things and Tribb ran into position.

And speaking of tinsel, Tinsley Reardon was no longer plucking her eyebrows, from what Parker could see. And neither was Courtney Wallace. And neither was Natalie Taylor, Parker's sixth best friend. All their eyebrows looked remarkably *natural,* just like Cricket's. A row of clones. At least they all were sitting in the front—the worst place on the planet to sit.

"What's with the Crick*ettes*?" Kiki asked, reading Parker's mind.

"They're seriously weirding me out," Plum said as she counted up the matching headbands and unplucked brows.

"We're *loving* the über-matchie thing. Aren't we?" Kenneth smiled in admiration. "It's very Diavolo-meets-Mar-a-Lago," he gushed. All the Lylas gave Kenneth the Hairy Eyeball. "But that's just me," he quickly added. "Me, myself, and moi." He laughed. "What do I know?"

"Hey, Court! Crick! Tins! Nat!" Parker forced herself to wave and smile—*noblesse oblige* and all that stuff.

"*Hello...*" Natalie enunciated.

"*And welcome!*" Courtney added dramatically.

The Crickettes laughed and then started whispering something to each other.

Parker blinked.

Hello? And Welcome?

What was that about? It must be a *seriously* super-bad feeling to think that somebody might wave and then start gossiping about you right behind your back and in front of your face at the same time. Parker felt sorry for people who'd do a thing like that. She looked down at the Crickettes again and tried to put it together. They wouldn't gossip about her...would they?

The bleachers filled up quickly as the game started. But, Parker noticed, it was like everything was upside-down. At the very bottom of the bleachers were the good people. People like Cosima, Suzanne, Felicia, Jake, Dylan, Brodie, Alex, and Sam.

People like that *never* sat in the front.

The Lylas had the top bleacher but then they were surrounded by the nobody people. The nobodies were sitting in the completely *wrong* place and now took up half of the second-to-top row. *(Ah, hello...where exactly were their shoes supposed to go now?)* Allegra Oliphant and the Einsteins blocked Kiki's view of everyone else—or more specifically, blocked everyone else's view of Kiki. And then all *those* nobody people were like invitations to more nobody people and soon every seat in the bleachers was filled. Good people at the bottom, bad people at the top, and the Lylas at, sort of, nowheresville.

"This is utter crap!" Kiki blurted. She stood up and marched down the bleachers. "Highly unamusing!" she mumbled as she went.

The rest of the Lylas followed her—mostly because none of them wanted to be left up there in North Kabumsville alone. They gathered by the water fountain around the corner of the school. Kiki huffed and puffed and scraped the mud off her heels. Parker slapped brown leaves out of Ikea's hair.

"The Big Game is so out," Kiki proclaimed with a flick of

grass and a clump of mud. "Can you *believe* the people sitting with us?"

The crowd screamed from the bleachers. The band burst into song. The Tigers had just scored a goal against Fox Chapel and Tribb and Beaver were doing the Hi-Fi-Ya in the field. Cricket waved. And Tinsley's whistle was hard to miss.

Parker took the Cherry Carmex out of her pocket and layered some on her lips.

"Are you going to kiss Tribb now?" Ikea asked with a mixture of hope and confusion.

"My lips are just chapped," she stated as she squeezed more from the tube. *Unfortunately.*

Something caught Parker's eye from down the stairs. It was James leaning silently beside a tree. His sweatshirt was zipped up close to his chin and his black jeans were worn out at the bottom edge where they dragged behind his shoes. It was really no different than how he usually dressed for school.

James would have blended into the scenery completely— nearly been invisible—if he hadn't been looking directly up at her. Parker could see those sharp blue eyes, even at fifty yards away. He peered out from behind the curls of his hair. He looked like he wanted something but she couldn't tell what.

Parker frowned. There was nothing high profile at all about James. He was *anti* profile, in fact. Just the kid who sat in the back of the auditorium. The kid who took weird photographs. The kid who had nothing to say. Just speaking to James knocked a person down a few notches on the populadder, if not off it completely. But there was something soft and comfortable about him. Something, Parker thought, that only she could see.

She didn't look away this time. Instead, she felt it all

unraveling in front of her eyes. School. Home. Her seat in the auditorium. Her spot on the bleachers. Her first kiss with Tribb—the only one she might have. And now this.

"Check out the stalkarazzi." Kiki nodded over toward James. "Does he take that camera wherever he goes?"

"What?" Parker flinched. She realized she was still putting on Carmex.

"*James!*" Kiki said again. "*Duh!* By that tree!"

"Oh..." Parker looked back down but James had disappeared. "Yeah."

"Earth to space cakes!" Kiki said. "Come in!"

• • •

So far, the Big Game was not going *at all* the way Parker expected.

The Tigers were winning against Fox Chapel of course, but that wasn't the point. It was impossible to be a shining example of what an eighth grader could be when nobody saw you being anything. When no one noticed you tossing autumn leaves into the air or checked out your golden, streakless tan. And honestly, Parker didn't even care about being an example of anything—she just wanted to be her regular self, her *popular* self, wearing the softest, most unbelievably pettable cashmere sweater and a one-of-a-kind vintage belt and really approachable jeans, but there was just no opportunity for it. The Lylas couldn't even sit down because sitting in the *wrong* seats was worse than sitting in *no* seats. So they just had to stand in front of the Gatorade table the whole time.

All they did was watch the frupping game!

"My dad thinks I can do better," Ikea blurted. She'd barely said a word since they'd gotten there.

"Pressure from the rental unit?" Plum questioned. "That's a newsflash."

"I mean, I don't know how I could do any better than 'Milestone Cases in Supreme Court History'…" Ikea fretted. She bit down so hard at the corner of her thumb, she nearly ripped her cuticle off. "I stayed up three nights in a row just practicing it."

"You *can't* do better," Plum assured her. "It was like the best webcast segment in the history of all webcast segments."

"It was totally faboush, darl!" Kiki exclaimed. "I had no idea that *Lovell v. Griffin* upheld the right of Jehovah's witnesses to distribute pamphlets without a license," she admitted. "I mean, that's good stuff."

"I hate the webcast," Ikea snarled. "It's the most useless, dumbest, stupidest thing in the entire world. And…" she ranted, "I looked up 'abecedarian'," she told them. "It means learning your *a, b, c*'s. Like being in kindergarten. It means even Ms. Hotchkiss thought it was pathetic."

"I hate the webcast too, Park," Plum confessed. "It's so…brown."

"I'm not doing it." Ikea stomped her Eliza B. flat on the grass.

"What about Yale?" Parker asked. "What about your dad?"

"I'm sick and tired of caring what my dad thinks. And Yale is just going to have to find some other reason to accept me," she said with a huff.

Parker stepped back. Ikea seemed so super-important right then. It was hard to imagine Yale, or any school, wouldn't accept someone with an amazingtude rating as high as Ikea's.

"If Ikea's not doing it…" Kiki looked at Parker but she didn't really have to finish the sentence. None of them did.

The sound of the cheers signaled another point for the Tigers. The game was coming to an end. The chances for the Acorns to recover were super-skinny to none (as if Parker even cared). Tribb and the rest of the team were doing spazzy victory dancing around the field: the Butter Churner, Tossing the Seeds, Raising the Roof, the Sprinkler. Parker was wondering why "not embarrassing" had never made it onto her EGB list.

She tried to get Tribb's attention, but it was pointless. Tribb was in Tigerland. No one else but the team existed.

"The webcast is *so* over," Plum said. Parker watched the game clock count down the last ten seconds. The buzzer signaled the game was done. "Isn't it, Parker?" she asked.

Tribb ran past them with the rest of the team. Parker pretended she was in the middle of a *very important* discussion (which was the truth) that couldn't be interrupted (which wasn't the truth). She did her I'm-here-but-I'm-not-desperate hair flip, but he was gone before she could tell if he saw it.

The webcast was ruining her life. She knew that for a fact.

"Somebody needs to tell Hotchkiss," Parker said.

"Don't look at *me*," Kiki declared.

"Hotchkiss gives me hives." Plum crossed her arms in front of her new *product*.

"I'll tell her," Ikea offered. "It's my fault we did it in the first place."

"It's not your fault we did it in the first place, Ike," Parker said. *It's my fault.* She knew what she had to do. "I'll talk to Hotchkiss on Monday."

Chapter 18

*T*HEY SAY THAT RIGHT before you die your life flashes in front of your eyes. And whoever *they* are, they're right.

Parker sat in the waiting room of Hotchkiss's office thinking about that very thing. But it wasn't her life flashing in front of her eyes; it was the fictional life of Chingachgook, the last of the Mohicans—the theme of the day playing over and over on the Super-Screen across the hall. There was something about waiting to talk to Hotchkiss while watching hi-definition 3-D tomahawks come flying at your head that seemed so apropos.

Parker looked up at the old wall clock over Alexander's head. Alexander was Hotchkiss's assistant. He guarded her door like a three-headed dog. They both waited for the second hand to move from the ten to the twelve, the precise moment that Hotchkiss would see her.

Tick. Tock. Tick. Tock—

"Parker Bell!" Hotchkiss opened her office door with a glossy smile. "Come in. Come in. My door is always open."

Ms. Hotchkiss's office was the most colorful, flowery, and cheerfully decorated spot in the school: taffeta drapes, butter-yellow walls with matching floral-print furniture, silk-covered Regency chairs, and a low gilt table with a vase of fresh flowers on it. The space was as confuzzling as say, Kiki shopping at Urban Outfitters—a type of environment and a type of person that just seemed so wrong when you stuck them together.

"Iced ginger ale?" Hotchkiss offered.

"No, thank you." Parker sat down on the striped slipper chair across from Hotchkiss. She felt a little Gretel entering a house made of gingerbread.

"And how *is* your lovely mother, Ellen?" Hotchkiss asked.

"She's lovely," Parker said politely.

"How nice to hear."

Hotchkiss took a sip of her own summery beverage, sat her endoskeleton back in her Regency chair, and waited for Parker to say something that might trigger the Terminator's internal programming to complete her mission of destroying the world one Wally at a time. She smiled.

Parker had spent the entire day Sunday practicing this speech in front of the mirror. But it really didn't matter because there was no way a person could prepare for the horror of the in-your-face, one-on-one moment with the actual living tissue. Plus there was nowhere to put her arms, because the slipper chair didn't have any. The Regency chair had all the arms a person could want. Hotchkiss was very calculating about the whole who-sat-where thing.

Okay. Now's the time. Just start talking.

"My classmates and I," Parker began, "would like to *thank* you for the webcast assignment. Er…opportunity." *Okay. Good start. Gracious. Smart. Responsible. Even the slip said Natural.* "We have *truly* learned so much about the world of online broadcasting and the internal workings of a production studio."

Hotchkiss was smiling, nodding and sipping. All good signs.

"*And...*" Parker continued. (Never say "But," no matter what you do. Parker read that in last month's article in *Lucky* on persuasive speaking. "But" was just an excuse. While "And" was filled with possibility. "And" was the word to use.) "*And...*" she said, "with the immense workload we hope to take on as we prepare for our collective futures *and* with Ikea setting her sites on Yale in five years *and* with Plum and all her art stuff *and* Kiki and all her...studying and things *and* with me, of course, and my interest in..." Parker tried to think. The idea came flying at her like tomahawks from a Super-Screen. "My interest in the Native American Peoples—"

"Native American Peoples?" Hotchkiss seemed suspicious of that last part. "Really?" She poured a ginger ale, plopped in three ice cubes, and pushed it toward Parker. (Which was fortunate because all this speaking was making Parker insanely thirsty.)

"Yes." Parker sipped the bubbly drink. "Native American Peoples..." She had to concentrate on swallowing. "Peoples whom I'm hoping to study more of." *Wait. That was wrong.* "*Of* whom I'm hoping to study more," she corrected.

"You can't get out of the webcast assignment, Parker, if that's where all this hoo-ha is headed," Hotchkiss stated.

"But...but...but..." *Oops...oops...oops.*

"You, Kiki, Plum, and Ikea," Hotchkiss continued, "have been given this assignment—this opportunity, as you phrased it—with the expectation that you will complete it." She made the word "expectation" sound like a poison that killed instantly upon contact. "And that *expectation* is non-negotiable," she said.

"But...but...but..."

Hotchkiss stood up from her chair and smoothed out the hem of her skirt.

"Fitz Orion has very specific intentions for the endowment monies he has so generously given to this school," Hotchkiss explained. So many of the words were sounding poisonous now, Parker thought she might just drop dead on the silk slipper chair. "So you girls are just going to have to live with it. And perhaps you'll find a way to incorporate your interest in the Native American Peoples." Hotchkiss walked over to her door. The clip-clop sound of her chic but sensible high heels was noticeably absent on her carpet. "Or perchance any of your *other* interests?"

Parker stood up. She stifled a burp from the ginger ale. She suddenly wished she knew how to belch the Alma Mater like Graham Henry did. Her life was over anyway. Eighth grade was ruined. The Lylas would never speak to her again. She'd leave Wallingford without ever being anyone important. Might as well go out with a bang. And a burp.

"You're a leader, Parker. Nearly everyone in your class looks up to you, even your best friends." Hotchkiss opened the door of her cheerful and sunny office. "A leader must decide what to do with her time. She can waste it wallowing in her problems. Or she can do something about them." Hotchkiss raised her cyborg eyebrows. "I'm sure you and your friends will find a way to make Wallingford Academy proud." (*We should have sent Plum*, Parker thought. At least *Plum* had the Hairy Eyeball. *She* only had indigestion.)

"Um...so—"

"Delightful of you to stop by." Hotchkiss smiled. "And *do* say hello to your mother."

Chapter 19

*G*YM CLASS WAS THE first chance Parker had to tell the Lylas about Hotchkiss. It was Monday gym, which meant field hockey (it also meant savory chicken pot pie or tofurkey with mashed potatoes and green beans almandine for lunch, which, after Kiki's webcast performance, every Wally well knew).

The Lylas hated field hockey because of the whole mouth guard sitch. Mouth guards, no matter who you were, what you did, or what you looked like, did not do anything good for a person. Ditto with pinnys. A bright yellow pinny just didn't do anything for anybody.

The four of them just stood in the corner of the field with their mouth guards tucked into the waistband of their hockey kilts, their phones stowed away inside their knee socks, and their pinnys tied into a knot at the bottom like that might make them look cuter. They held their sticks in front of them, occasionally popping out and moving around to make it look like they were actually playing. Parker still couldn't muster the courage to speak. Finally Kiki cleared her throat.

"Well, I guess you're not expelled *a la mo*," Kiki guessed, "because you'd have to be thoroughly daft to be expelled and play field hockey anyway. Just for kicks." She leaned on her stick as the rest of the gym class fought for the goal down the field. "Expelled and hockey is like a double negative. Like wide wale corduroy."

"That's a triple negative," Plum observed. "Wide. Whale. *And* Corduroy."

"Plus," Ikea pointed out, "it's *wale*. Without the *h*."

"Whatevs." Kiki made the big *W* over her forehead. "Parker's still not expelled. Which means…what, exactly?"

Ikea volleyed her hockey stick left and right like she was really playing. Except for the fact that she was fifty yards from the action, it was fairly convincing. While Ikea was nearly perfect at everything else, she was a total spazette in gym. She'd learned how to work with what she had and look good doing it—a Lylas credo if there ever was one.

"Hotchkiss nearly poisoned me," Parker told them. She lowered her eyes, knowing she'd failed her friends. "It was terrible. I couldn't get us out of it."

"Buggers!" Kiki stomped her cleats. "I *knew* it!"

"What are we going to do?" Plum asked.

"Move to a new town." Parker said. *At least that's what I'm doing.*

"How about London?!" Kiki suggested, only half-joking. They all watched as Cricket ran quickly down the field and, just as she got within the limits of the striking circle, passed the ball to Cosima, who scored a goal. Cricket's shiny hair swayed back and forth as she ran. Her matchie-matchie headband kept it all neatly away from her face. Her dark, natural eyebrows made her perfect, corn-on-the-cob teeth look even whiter. (P.S.—Even though natural eyebrows were now in according to this month's *Teen Vogue,* they were still *so out* according to the Lylas.)

Coach Payne blew her whistle. All the Crickettes were

jumping up and down with excitement. Their leader had so generously let someone else score. Yes, the ugly truth reared its ugly head: Cricket Von Wielding was truly a shining example of what an eighth grader could be.

"What do they all see in her anyway?" Plum stared.

"She's *only* the governor's daughter," Ikea reminded her.

"A veritable supernova of *meh*," Kiki said.

"She has three-hundred-and-two Friends," Ikea told them. "That's only ninety-four fewer than Parker."

"No!" Kiki could barely contain herself.

"I have a Friend from Christmas Island," Parker reminded everyone. *That counts for something. Right?*

"Nice." They all nodded.

"Festive," Kiki said.

Pathetic, actually, Parker thought.

"And, I know you're going to hate this, Keek, but…" Ikea pulled her phone out from her sock and turned it on, "they started a Fans of the Lunch Menu Group."

"Really?" Kiki was surprised and more than a bit flattered. "A fan club?"

"Don't call your agent just yet." Plum peered at Ikea's screen.

Kiki and Parker gathered around Ikea's phone. The sound of video was tinny and barely audible but the top ten hit was familiar enough to fill in the blanks.

"'Ain't Nuffin but a Jam Thang'?" Kiki was in shock.

"Hump D. Dump." Parker nodded cautiously.

It was an awful sight. Someone in the group had superimposed Kiki's head on DJ Jazzy Jeremy's body. Kiki's oversized face was frozen into an awkward position while Jazzy Jeremy showed off his most bewildering freestyling to the Hump D. Dump beat.

"It's pretty realistic." Ikea couldn't help but admire the technology. Kiki gasped and went pale. Parker rushed quickly beside her.

Coach Payne's whistle blew. "Girls!" She yelled loudly from the other end of the field. Ikea deftly slid her phone back into her sock. She made it look like she was stretching. "I see the wheel spinning but the hamster looks dead!"

Parker barely heard her. All she heard was the sound of the Crickettes snickering.

Part

III

Semper Veritas

Chapter 20

$\mathcal{K}$ IKI SAT SILENTLY IN the middle of the comfy couch at La Coppa Coffee, her pupils dilated and fixed like she was rehearsing to play the lead in a glamorous zombie movie. Plum had to hold her tea for her because Kiki had already crushed two of them. Her legs were covered in the scalding remnants of two grande English Breakfasts. Kiki hadn't even felt the pain.

Ikea was looking at the fans of the Lunch Menu Group on her phone. Parker snuck a peek over her shoulder and read the painful (and growing) list of members. The group linked directly to the webcast itself.

The feeling was pure panic. Parker just wanted to reach into Facebook and yank the whole thing out, but she couldn't. It wasn't her home page. What could she do?

"So this is what humiliation feels like." Plum groaned.

"Carnage." Ikea agreed. Parker shut her eyes tightly.

Kiki sighed. "I can't believe I horked in gym class."

"At least you got to go to the nurse's office," Plum said.

"At least you didn't have your head cut off and stuck on Jeremy Landis's body!"

At least you don't have to leave Wallingford and go to be a noof at Fox Chapel Middle School! Parker wanted to scream. But she couldn't tell them now. They would have felt like she was leaving on purpose. She couldn't let them down—she had to get them out of it. *She* had to get out of it.

All four of them were squeezed onto the couch. The only way it seemed to feel any better was being squished all together like a big wad of Play-Doh from four different cans—at least they were in the ugly mess together.

"I guess we can't call backsies." Plum shook her head at Ikea's small but devastating screen.

"Remember Samantha Mazzafundo's video of herself singing 'Can I Have This Dance'?" Ikea powered down and put the phone away.

"Anyone can Google 'Mazzafundo' and see it," Plum said. "For all eternity."

Parker tried her best to think of a solution but her mind was painfully blank.

"What's happening to us, Park?" Plum asked.

"I don't know." Parker didn't have a clue. Her (former) ninth, tenth, eleventh, and twelfth best friends were members of the group. She felt sick. All her work had amounted to nothing.

"Everything was going great and next thing you know…" Plum took a sip of Kiki's lukewarm tea. "Arthur the janitor is down on the field with a bucket and bag of sawdust."

"Very funny." Kiki took her tea. "It was a perfectly natural reaction."

"A melt-down is a gateway toward a total transformation," Ikea announced plainly. They all looked at her in disbelief. Ikea could get so annoyingly empowered sometimes. "It is, you guys!" she assured them. "It's been proven."

"GirlPower is like the last thing we need right now, Ike," Plum said.

But Parker kept listening. Ikea was smarter than anyone she knew. *Besides, it's not like anyone else had any brilliant ideas.*

"Maybe we have to open the door," Ikea explained, "take the Gateway, and walk boldly toward Self-Empowerment." She smiled slyly.

"That's the most *RYE-dik-u-luz* thing anyone has ever said! Ever!" Kiki raised her voice. "Like in their entire lives!"

"Uh, hello?" Plum said. "What about 'I do' to McDweebs in second grade?"

Parker winced. Things were getting out of control. This was serious rule breakage: *Never mention the arriage-may in front of Iki-Kay. Never!*

"Stop, you guys," Parker demanded. Super-pissiness was not helping find a solution to the problem. "No ideas are bad ideas," she reminded them. "It's a rule. Remember?"

Ikea dropped her head and Kiki attempted a very careful sip of her tea. Plum squinted at the front door of La Coppa Coffee as it opened. A rush of fall leaves kicked up outside.

"Check out who it is." Plum pointed over to Graham Henry, who was waiting in line with his mother. Ikea looked up. "The Belch-Maestro."

Graham looked over at the Lylas and gave them a devilish smile.

"That kid is a serious case." Kiki said. "He gives Wallingford Academy a bad name."

Parker's eyes grew wide. She got goose bumps all over her arms. "What did you say, Keek?"

"About what?" Kiki sipped her tea.

"About the kid!" Parker said. "You were saying, he gives Wallingford Academy a bad name…"

"Parker, I really can't do the fake super-nice thing today—"

"But he does, Kiki!" Parker interrupted. "He gives Wallys a bad name!" Parker started doing the Happy Wiggle (another Lylas move). "I love you, Graham Henry!" she shouted.

Kiki struggled to free herself of the couch and put some distance between herself and Parker's freakish outburst.

"Don't you get it, Keek?" Parker said breathlessly. "Great leaders don't sit there and wallow in their problems. They fix them." She felt like tropical punch Pop Rocks were going off in her head. "And Graham gives Wallys a bad name!" She wrapped her arms around Kiki and squeezed. "You're brilliant!"

"She is?" Plum looked confused.

"I am?" Kiki looked even more confused.

"Ohhhh…" Ikea was the first to get it. "We're love *love* loving it!"

"Hotchkiss said that she was sure we'd do something that would make the school proud…" Parker painted her vision for them.

"So what if we do something that *won't* make the school proud…" Ikea continued.

"Something she won't show," Parker explained.

"Like the DVD won't work or something?" Now Plum was really confused.

"Not something she *can't* show…" Ikea told Plum.

"Something she *won't* show. As in *ever*." Parker said. "Something that would give Wallingford a bad name."

Plum's grin grew until it filled half her face. "If we do the worst show, like the *baddest* show ever…" She finally figured it out. "She'll have to fire us."

"Positutely," Parker said. "And everything will be back the way it was before we started doing the crummy webcast."

Kiki smiled wickedly. "I *am* brilliant."

"Hotchkiss will just have to give it to someone else." Parker smiled too. "She'll have no choice."

"The Einsteins," Kiki said.

"Exactly," Parker agreed.

"Allegra Oliphant will be *soooo* excited." Ikea did the Birdie.

"Totally! So, like we're doing something completely nice." Parker said.

"Like an example."

"For the whole school to follow."

"Très perfect idea."

"Fantabulous."

Ikea was right. All they needed was a little GirlPower.

"To the worst show ever." They turned toward each other and clinked friendship rings. "To the worst show."

For the first time in weeks, it once again felt great to be a Lyla.

• • •

Parker taped up pictures of dresses and hairdos for Fall Sosh on the wall next to her desk. She organized them in order of preference and color. Something blue, she thought. *Maybe?* Or canary yellow, which looks great with a fresh tan. She opened her computer to its most frequented website but she didn't check her requests box or compare her Facebook Friend count with everyone else's or search for the new app that would animate her profile pic. Instead she focused on the blank box at the top of the screen.

What's your status right now?

She wasn't answering the question for anyone but herself today. It was *her* status. Nothing anyone said, no group anyone else belonged to, no wall anyone wrote on, would change that. She looked over at the pictures of dresses again. She pulled her favorite one down: full length, pale blue with a really great neckline. She circled the store where it came from.

A mischievous grin came across her face. It was a brilliant plan, if she didn't say so herself.

What's your status right now?

Parker is...not giving up.

Chapter 21

HE FUNNY THING WAS, the Lylas spent even more time working on the horrible version of *Wallingford Academy Today* than they had on the first one. It was like bad ideas were way more fun to think about than good ones. It didn't even seem like work to Parker—it felt just like regular Lylas stuff: how it all was supposed to be again. With no time to lose, everything was getting back on track.

"The beige, off-beige set has to go." Plum sat in front of the mirror at the World of Beauty and painted a blue lightning bolt on her cheek with liquid eyeliner. Plum's sense of style had grown bolder along with the size of her chest. Thanks to the patented technology of American Coquette, she was now a full size B. The undershirts were gone.

"I completely agree. Has to go immediately." Parker tried to wipe some fugly mauve lipstick off, not realizing it was the kind of lipstick that's supposed to remain on one's lips barring everything except an apocalypse.

Plum finished her lightning bolt, put some nail polish remover on a cotton ball, and handed it to Parker.

"Maybe something that makes you sick just looking at it." Ikea combed clear eyebrow tamer gel onto each of her brows.

"Like Levi 501s?" Kiki suggested. She powdered her nose with Terra-cotta Mineral bronzer. Everyone looked over at her. "What?" she asked. "I can't help it. 501s make me sick, all right?"

• • •

Plum continued to think about it the next day when the Lylas were doing homework on the ground floor of the Hunt Memorial Library. "Maybe...neon or*ange*." She rhymed the word with "door-hinge" just like Mr. Lewis, the art teacher, had. "Like a... *discotheque.*" She remembered his description of her Cézanne still-life drawing. "One feels *ill*, when one looks at it," she quoted.

"What's a disco-theck?" Kiki whispered from across the library table.

Ikea did a Google image search on her phone. She turned the screen toward everyone and smiled.

"Oh...." They all nodded knowingly. "A *discotheque!*"

Ikea enlarged the image.

"Très perrrfect," Plum purred.

"That's so *wrong*." Parker grinned as Ikea scrolled.

"*No cell phones* in the library, Miss Bentley!" Ms. Fenderson, the librarian, dropped the yellow slip on the table. Ikea's name was right up top.

"My first yellow slip!" Ikea beamed with pride. The plan was working already.

• • •

The next afternoon they went to the Hat & Scarf department at Langdon's.

"I think I should do a piece about the fact that there are only nine African American students at Wallingford Academy when there should be *fifty-three point six!*" Ikea announced.

Kiki picked out a black furry hat. She centered the big thing on Ikea's head.

"That's eighty-three point-four percent less than there should be…" Ikea unbuttoned her navy cardigan and tied it loosely around her hips. "…given the statistical breakdown of the country."

"Totally *en* agreement, Ike." Kiki surveyed the look she'd picked out. "Proportion is everything."

Parker and Plum folded their arms in front of their chests and squinted at Ikea's head. Kiki tucked Ikea's smooth, shiny hair up under the hat so it seemed like the mass of black fluff *was* Ikea's hair. Parker used the Clipboard app on her phone to take notes. The ideas were flowing so fast, she could barely get them all down. Ten folders had already been filled.

Plum sketched Ikea and her hat in pencil in her notebook.

"Wallys of color are nearly invisible! At our school. At *my* school." Ikea was so mad the fur on her head was shaking. "Just look at my friend, Divya Venkataraghavan."

"Who?" Plum asked.

"Exactly." Ikea turned around and looked at herself in the mirror. Her hazel eyes registered horror. Kiki stared over Ikea's shoulder.

"I don't think you should wear that hat in front of the Yale admissions committee," Plum said.

"No way," Parker agreed.

"Your dad would have a nip fit if he saw you right now," Plum added.

Kiki nodded. "Completely."

"Hmm." A smile spread across Ikea's face. "Fierce, right?!"

• • •

"I'm so not doing the lunch menu again," Kiki declared as

they walked through the Orion computers retail store Saturday morning. Liam Davies's new music video played on all the Super-Screens. "Can't I do something spiff, like be a guest celebrity or something?" She leaned against the display counter and flipped through her magazine.

"You're not really a celebrity, Keek," Parker said. "Sorry to break it to you."

Kiki picked up the new black glitter case Plum was buying and held it up to her ear just to try it. Plum was preoccupied with her phone, tapping out something with her thumbs. Parker's phone buzzed in her tote. She looked at the ID—it was Plum. But Plum was standing across from her, less than five feet away.

EGB. DN'T TRN AROUND.

Parker froze. She looked up at Plum. They couldn't even exchange secret signals because the target was too close. Plum just moved her eyes back and forth toward the tabletop speaker section of the store—obviously the 10–20 on the EGB.

Another message arrived from Plum, the answer to Parker's unasked next question.

UR HAIR IS G2G. LYLAS

0: -)

Soon all the Lylas except Parker had seen Tribb and they were all eye-rolling it toward the speakers. Parker's back was still toward him. She quickly relaxed her body posture, fluffed her hair out and began talking like she was in the middle of a very important conversation that had nothing at all to do with Tribb and his whereabouts.

"And then after I hit that party," Parker said, "I really wasn't in the mood for another one—I mean, it was getting so late." She laughed once (the perfect amount of times).

"Oh, I *know*," Kiki ran with it, "how many fabuloso parties can a girl do in one weekend?"

"Hey." Tribb walked up to the group. He was wearing his sweats and his hair looked recently slept on. He smelled less like Outdoor Fresh fabric softener sheets and more like socks.

"Wow!" Parker acted like she was surprised. "So funny to see you here." The store was filled with people their age and tons of Wallys. In truth, it wasn't all that funny to see anybody you knew there. It was practically a hangout.

"Yeah." Tribb nodded. "I don't even know why I'm here. I already own almost everything in here." He laughed.

She laughed.

They all laughed.

The Liam Davies video had finished playing on the Super-Screens and an old Rebels video came on. Sid Stryker hadn't changed all that much in the decade he'd been renovating his mansion but Parker had. She wished she could turn back the clock.

Tribb looked at Parker like he was about to ask her something. *This is it! The big question—about to be popped!* The rest of the Lylas turned away like they were instantly focused on something more interesting than Tribb asking Parker to Fall Social. (They weren't.) Parker tried to hold her expression still but she kept blinking uncontrollably.

Tribb nodded over to the Super-Screen like he'd only just noticed it was there. "The Rebels rock..." He pointed.

Parker turned around. Sid Stryker's face filled the screen. "The Rebels. Yeah. No. Totally," she agreed. "Completely rock."

There was an odd noise in the background. Someone singing completely off tune. Parker looked past Tribb. James was standing there in the music player area trying out earphones. He was singing so loudly to the music he was listening to that it drowned out Tribb completely. His whole body bobbed up and down as if nobody else was there in the store. Parker laughed when she saw him.

"The bootleg version of 'Live Before You Die' is so fresco..." Tribb kept talking even though Parker was losing it watching James. "I can't even find it on Limewire..."

Parker remembered Tribb was speaking. "It's what?" She tried to focus.

"Limewire," Tribb repeated. "I can't even find it."

"Apple bottom jeans...boots with the fur..." James sang.

"Oh yeah?" Parker worked to key in on Tribb but it was pretty difficult given James's performance. She bit her lip to keep away a laugh attack. *Had Tribb asked her to Fall Social?* "You what?"

"Shawty got low, low, low, low, low, low..."

Plum was laughing too.

Tribb looked over at James. "Isn't that the AV guy?" He seemed annoyed. James took his earphones off and checked the price tag. He didn't see Parker or Tribb or any of the Lylas before he left. Parker tried to hold it together as Tribb continued. "Can you believe that toolshed?"

Once James was gone, Parker suddenly remembered that

Tribb was supposed to be asking her something. "What was that?" she asked.

Tribb ruffled the top of his hair and looked back again at the front door. "So, I guess I better be going." He put his hand in his pocket and locked his knees.

Parker gulped down her disappointment. "Oh."

"I'll see you at school." He waved.

"Sure." Parker scooped the front of her hair and let it fall gracefully back down on the face. So much for the big moment. "See you at school."

Chapter 22

HE *WALLINGFORD ACADEMY TODAY* studio was starting to look more like a bustling frontline war room than the dark, heavily decked-out former language studies classroom that it was. Parker took over an entire corner for herself and transferred everyone's show ideas from the Clipboard app onto two old giant chalkboards and a wall-sized cork board Arthur the janitor had found for her in storage. Parker could have used a Genius Pen and simply uploaded all the ideas into the air and let them dangle there like a virtual chandelier, but some things just made more sense when you could stick *actual* stickies all over the place (gasp!).

It was agreed that Kiki could hold the newly created title of *Wallingford Academy Today* Costume Designer. (The only way to get her to stop talking about outfits was to get her doing them.) She turned a large storage closet off the back of the edit studio into a room she called Tea & Wardrobe. She brought in racks of clothes, stacks of mags, a velvet curtain to get dressed behind, a tin of English Breakfast tea, and an electric teapot. She "borrowed" a small table from the library, a topiary tree from the foyer, and brought in the pink satin chair from her own closet to receive guests (namely Kenneth, who had nothing better to do after school than sit in Kiki's pink chair and goss about stuff 'n' junk while sipping tea from a dainty cup).

Plum brought in dozens of paintbrushes, buckets of bright "door-hinge" paint, and a Prius-sized disco ball she'd made out of her mother's Pilates ball, paper-mache, and glue-on mirror tiles. She'd found a kaleidoscope strobe light and a Halloween fog machine at Party Plus, a white plastic living room set at Ikea (the store, not the person), and two silver chairs shaped like huge hands in her grandmother's basement.

She'd also instantly become one of Ms. Fenderson's favorite students by submitting a Librarian Research Inquiry into "discotheques." It must've been the first Librarian Research Inquiry Ms. Fenderson had received since the discovery of the World Wide Web. Plum had never been anyone's favorite student before and didn't even get in trouble for chomping watermelon gum in the library.

Being bad had its advantages.

Ikea hardly took up any room at all in the studio. She sat cross-legged in one of Plum's silver hand-chairs with a stack of Wallingford Academy yearbooks, her phone and a super-serious look on her face. Occasionally she'd walk back into Tea & Wardrobe, look through Kiki's clothes racks, and come back singing to herself. If you asked her what she was doing, she'd say "Ohhh, nothing…" like the same way you'd say it if you just smooched off your Cherry Carmex with your EGB behind the gym (not that Parker would know—she was so busy with the webcast, she'd hardly seen Tribb much less smooched him).

Neither James nor McDweebs cared about whether they were doing the old version of the show or the new one— neither of them really gave a flying flip about losing their Wally status because they had none. McDweebs was just excited to spend quality drool-time with the Orion 2000 XZ.

He had become the hero of the GameCube Olympians just for touching the XZ. As long as it meant that McDweebs could flip the beepie-buttons, turn the thingamabobbies, fine tune the knoobly knobs on the million dollar machine, and be within ten feet of his quasi-wife, life was good by him.

James, as usual, was working his own grind. He didn't really care what the show was about; making it look cool on film was the only thing that mattered to him. He would try a thousand different test shots with the digital camcorder, then inspect the playback carefully with McDweebs. Sometimes he'd suddenly burst out of his chair, grab his camera, run back into the studio, and start filming something again.

To Parker, it didn't seem like James was trying anything different than he had just a minute before, but James would nod and tap his foot like he was keeping time with his explosion of ideas. He'd then race back to McDweebs in the edit suite with the memory card to see what he had done.

But whatevs. Parker simply tried to keep the mission on track. The sooner they'd get kicked off the assignment, the sooner eighth grade (aka life) would get back to normal.

Even though Plum's set wasn't finished yet, Parker was amazed at how James made it come more and more alive on the wide XZ Super-Screen monitor with each new pass of his camera. The set looked insane but Parker liked what James was doing anyway. It was weird spending this much time watching somebody create something. It was almost like being really great friends with someone…except *not*. He didn't get that they were trying to sabotage the whole thing. Or did he?

James's face always lit up when he watched the footage on the monitor. His ice blue eyes scanned the screen from left to right as he studied his work. Even though envy was strictly against Lylas rules, Parker caught herself noticing how easy things seemed for James. He didn't worry about how he dressed or what he said or didn't say. He did whatever he felt like doing and never stressed out. He didn't seem to care what anyone else thought. Parker couldn't even begin to imagine what that feeling was like.

• • •

"I really like the part where it looks like the chair is moving closer to the camera. It's très cool," Parker told James one afternoon. (*Lavishly complimenting the other person's new thing* felt like it should extend to stuff besides clothes and totes.)

"I wanted to get a feeling of movement without falling into the whole hand-held trap," he said excitedly as he watched the playback, "so I changed the zoom setting—and tried the telephoto lens to see if I could get a compression effect without all that old school distortion."

Parker furrowed her eyebrows and laughed. "I have no idea what you're talking about," she said. "But I still like it."

James smiled, pushing his floppy hair away from his eyes.

"How about a quick reverse cut here without the fade?" McDweebs asked James. "Something like this…"

With the push of a button McDweebs spliced two pieces of James's footage together so that they became something new. The area James had filmed—the tiny, orange and silver set that was just a few feet away, Plum's work d'art—now seemed like an endless world, like a faraway planet that no one had discovered yet. Parker's heart beat fast as she watched.

"Illmatic." McDweebs admired the result.

"Wicked illmatic," James agreed.

• • •

147

No one had any idea what Ikea was up to with her segment—it was top secret or something. Parker crossed her fingers that it wasn't going to be so super-smart that it made everything else look too good. She sat in one of Plum's silver hand chairs and scribbled on her Wallingford Academy notebook. The worst part of it? Parker had been so busy with the show she hadn't even had time to plan for Fall Sosh. It was only a week away and she hadn't practiced her updo or her walk down the stairs. She hadn't even peeked out the studio window for weeks. She didn't feel like herself anymore. Parker filled in the letters of the motto part of the school seal on the front of the notebook.

"What about 'Good night and have a pleasant tomorrow'?" She suggested a closing line for the show to James. "I think someone famous closed their show out like that." Parker could already tell he didn't like it. "Or maybe, 'Stay tuned for more newsiness'?" she asked him. "Or," Parker wondered aloud. "'May the good news be yours'?"

"I dunno…" James pulled up the other silver hand chair and sat beside Parker while they thought. "Nobody at Wallingford really cares about the news anyway," he said.

Plum tested the spin speed of her disco ball with a switch. The tiny mirrored lights swirled around the room. James's eyes sparkled in their reflection.

"How about just 'Bye bye'?" Parker asked as she colored. "I mean, it's totally to the point. Right?"

"I guess…" James agreed (sort of). He pulled the hood of his sweatshirt over his head and rested his chin on his hand. *He hated it. How obvs can you be?*

"But it's a snooze cruise," Parker admitted.

"Z Town." They both laughed.

She looked at the letters she was coloring in. "How about *Semper Veritas?*" she asked as she filled in the oval inside the *a*.

"Stay true..." He repeated the phrase in English. "You know, I don't think anybody even knows what that means."

Parker nodded. "That's what Plum said too." Then she remembered Kiki's suggestion. "But *maybe* I have a better idea" She grinned. "Excusez moi, all." Kenneth interrupted the studio work.

"Attention!" Kenneth repeated until everyone stopped what they were doing. Plum turned off the disco ball. Kiki stopped sewing. "May I introduce..." Kenneth said loudly, "the girl most likely *not* to be accepted at Yale..."

"*Or Princeton.*" Ikea's muffled voice yelled out from behind the velvet curtain in Tea & Wardrobe. "...*But possibly still Harvard,*" she added.

Kenneth made a drum roll sound with his fingers.

"The Fabulouz Ikea Bentley..." Kenneth announced.

The curtain rustled, then opened. When Ikea walked onto the set it was as if an explosion went off, blowing out all the walls of the studio, the school, the doors, the ceiling...leaving only the bit of floor she was standing on.

Parker's eyes worked their way from the bottom up. Ikea's knee-high, lace-up boots were rugged and thick and made out of the same kid-suede as the A-shaped mini-skirt that framed her sturdy hips. Her tight T-shirt (definitely not from Lilly's in East Hampton) showed off everything there was to show. Over it, she wore an opened jean vest with a half-dozen political pins stuck to both pockets. Dipped in soapy water, her hoop earrings could have blown bubbles the size of pizzas into the air.

And her hair, her *hair,* was not shiny and straight at all. At first Parker thought it might be the hat from Langdon's, but it wasn't. Ikea's hair was all her own. It was natural. Frizzy. Untamed. Massive. It circled around her head and shook like the fur hat had. It was an Afro in all its glory. Simple as that. And it was big enough to put any '70s movie to shame.

But it wasn't the boots, or the suede mini-skirt, or the pizza-sized earrings, or the pins that were controversial enough to start a file on her with the FBI—or the fact that not one single thing on her was monogrammed or pink or made out of ribbon—it wasn't even Queen Ike's dangerously large new hairdo that caused Parker's jaw to drop to the floor...It was the thing Ikea *wasn't* wearing, well the *two* things, left and right, that made everyone just about lose the plot.

"Is it too much?" Ikea asked.

Parker blinked. She coughed. Nearly choked. But Plum stated the obvious for everyone:

"Ikea! Your eyes are *brown!*"

Chapter 23

*I*T WAS LATE AND the studio was quiet. Everyone but Parker and James had gone home. James put away the last of the equipment. The sound of the locks closing on his camera case sounded so final. All that was left now was to turn it in to Hotchkiss and wait to get dragged into her office and get fired. By tomorrow this horrible chapter of eighth grade would be over—Parker just had to keep reminding herself that.

"Here you go." James handed Parker the copy of the webcast.

The DVD seemed so small for something that took so long. Parker grabbed her tote and slung it around her shoulder. She tried to smile.

James gathered his heavy backpack, his personal camera, and a flat box of photography paper. He slipped the box into his backpack and heaved the whole thing up over his shoulder.

As he shut off the last of the lights and Parker locked the door behind them, she couldn't help but shiver. The school was dark and empty. The sound of Arthur's enormous floor-shine machine whirring somewhere above them was all they heard.

"It's so creepy in here when it's late," she muttered. She didn't want to walk up to Hotchkiss's door all by herself. Every horror movie that ever took place in a school filled her mind.

Blood-thirsty vampires (*not* the cute ones) could be lurking just about anywhere.

James lifted his hood up and nodded. "I was going that way anyway," he said. Parker was über-relieved.

Together they walked back down the hallway, past the dark row of Orion Super-Screens, past the bomb shelter entrance and the two old phone booths, past the nurse's office and the lower level of the Hunt Memorial Library, toward the stairwell that led up to the empty office and the door that the DVD would slide under.

James stopped in front of the door to the stairwell.

"Parker, I know you and your friends really hated doing this…" he said, "but I'm really happy we got the chance to work together. I thought it was really fun." James gave her a warm, boyish smile, one she remembered from their dance together around the maypole. "But I know you'll be pretty glad after tomorrow. Hey, you're *Parker Bell*." He pushed open the door. "You have better things to do with your life."

"I don't have a dad, you know," Parker heard herself admit. She wasn't sure why she told him—she just felt like she needed to say the words, like she wanted James to know. "Sometimes it just doesn't feel like I really deserve any of this….being popular, having a lot of people looking up to me," she said. "I'm really just a nobody who pretends to be a somebody."

Parker took a deep breath. She smiled even though she felt like crying. James just listened. There was something about saying the words out loud to James that made it feel like it wasn't as big of a deal as it was.

James set down his heavy backpack on the landing.

"And I don't only know how to take pictures of the lunch

ladies serving up macaroni and cheese, by the way," he told her. Parker shook her head. She'd almost forgotten that question she asked him on the first day they were in the studio.

James pulled out his box of photography paper, slid out a print at the top of the pile and handed it to her. Parker held the print carefully. Even in the darkness of the stairwell she could see.

"That's me!" Parker stared.

Parker studied her own face. It must have been the split second after she noticed James standing beside the tree at the Big Game but before he'd disappeared. Her hair was swept across her forehead and framed her eyes like long tendrils. Her body was turned in a way where you couldn't tell if she was leaving or she'd just arrived. She didn't look perfect, like the cover of the magazine pose she'd practiced or the Academy Award acceptance speech—but it just seemed like James captured something private about her through his lens.

Something not so terrible.

"I've been meaning to give it to you," James told her. "I like the way you look…" His eyes met hers. "I mean in the photo," he corrected. "The composition and stuff."

"Sure. Yeah." Parker laughed. "The composition is great." She tucked the print into her tote. It fit neatly into the side. *It was good that totes were still so in,* she thought. "Thanks."

James lifted his backpack back up and they walked the rest of the way up toward Hotchkiss's office door.

"Are you going to Fall Social on Saturday?" Parker asked without thinking. *Dumb. Dumb. It was a dumb question, Parker!* James would think she was asking him to go with her and that's so not what she meant—

"Sure," James said. "I'm the AV guy, remember? Can't have a party without me." He smiled. "Who'd work the sound?"

He pushed open the door to the first floor. The sound of Arthur's machine drowned everything else out. Parker was instantly embarrassed in the light. Her face felt hot—she knew she must have been bright red.

"I thought you kids just about disappeared down there." Arthur the janitor yelled. His voice vibrated as he worked his oversized machine. Like magic, he left a trail in his wake: the floor behind him was shinier than the floor in front.

"Nah," Parker shouted above the noise. She held up the DVD in the blank jewel case. "Just finishing things up," she said. *Finishing things up,* she thought again. Why did she feel so bad when the news was so good?

"I'll be watching tomorrow." Arthur held up his iPhone. The oldest man in the world…with the same phone as Parker had. How weird was that? "I subscribe to the show," he said as he moved on to the rest of the hall.

"Thanks, Arthur." Parker smiled. "Our one subscriber," she whispered to James.

James adjusted his heavy backpack on his shoulder. "I gotta run, Parker. My mom's waiting outside."

"Oh. Sure. Me too." Parker stood at Ms. Hotchkiss's door holding the jewel case. This was it, she thought. She'd push it under the door and it would all be over. Simple as that.

"You okay?" James asked as he shuffled toward the front.

"Yeah." Parker smiled at him as he opened the front door and disappeared into the night. "Totally okay," she repeated.

Parker knelt down to the narrow crack beneath the door and put the side of her face on the floor. The space was just tall enough to let the case slip through to the other side of the door. She tried to look through to the office but her face couldn't get close enough with her nose in the way.

She felt the vibration of the building like it was alive.

With just one flick of her index finger, it was done.

Chapter 24

*T*HE VERY FRONT ROW of the Freeman Auditorium was a whole different place than the very back row, or even the second-to-back row, of the eighth grade section. They truly were the very worst seats in the whole room, but they were the only seats that were left. The eighth grade section was completely full. Unless Parker turned around, she couldn't see anyone (as in Tribb) and anyone (as in Tribb) couldn't see her. (Well, except for the back of her head, which meant, if she had any plans for staying there more than this single Matin, she would need to contemplate a whole new hairstyle. But she didn't. So she wouldn't.)

She tried not to let her embarrassment show but she thought some of it was probably leaking out. She was embarrassed for all four of them.

I will never have to sit here again. We will never have to sit here again.

She repeated the words in her head.

"Could this be any more humilifying?" Kiki asked with an audible puff of air. "I can't *believe* that it's Fall Sosh tomorrow, only the first black tie event of the school year, and we're sitting *here!*" she complained. "And why doesn't anyone have my haircut yet?"

Parker kept turning around toward the back of the

auditorium. She was sure she'd see Hotchkiss at any moment, storming through the foyer and down the aisle like Miss Gulch in a Kansas tornado, pointing a finger at Parker and signaling that she wanted to see her immediately.

But there was no sign of the headmistress.

Parker couldn't understand why Hotchkiss hadn't summoned them to her office already. She was sure Alexander would have gathered the production staff all together in the waiting room before first bell, but he hadn't. And if Alexander wasn't going to find them *before* first bell, he would have definitely sent a note into Latin Studies requesting their immediate presence—he knew all their schedules. They weren't hard to find. If not Latin Studies, she thought, then biology. If not biology, then French. Alexander even *saw* Parker doing her Virtual Humanities homework in the library before Matin. He could have quietly come over to her and whispered in her ear: *"Ms. Hotchkiss's office. Now."*

But it was Matin and they hadn't been fired yet. It made no sense. Parker chomped on about a dozen cinnamint Tic-Tacs as they waited. Ikea had tamed her new Afrofabulous hair into two pouffy ponytails on either side of her head. Parker thought they looked like ice skate pom-poms with grosgrain ribbons around them.

Ikea bit her fingernails. "My dad's in court today," she said nervously looking around. "He won't be here." She craned her neck again. "Like pretty much for sure."

Parker nodded. "Like *no way* he's coming."

"I thought we'd already be dead by now," Plum said.

"I'm sure Hotchkiss has something worse than death planned," Kiki suggested.

"We're just getting *fired*, you guys," Parker reminded them. "Not executed."

"What if she actually decides to show it?" Ikea asked hesitantly.

"She's *not* going to show it." Parker pinky swore. "Can you imagine Hotchkiss *actually* showing your segment?! Or Kiki's lunch menu?! Or Plum's discotheque?"

"Umm yeah, *no way*," Plum agreed.

"Not happening."

"Negatory." They all nodded.

"Do you think we went too far?" Ikea asked.

"Absolutely."

"Completely."

Parker allowed herself a smile of satisfaction. "Well, that *was* the point."

"Hey." Tribb, Kirby, and Beaver slid in to the seats two rows behind them. Parker turned around but not so much that her neck got all crinkly and made a double-chin (she'd practiced, and rejected, that pose many times). Somehow, Tribb had gotten even more quantumly gorgeous since soccer season started. He'd look so hawt in his tux. Parker's stomach was instantly tied in a knot.

Plum sat back up straight in her chair. Her new 32 B Fantasias really stood out.

"Hey…" Parker completely forgot to have a more clever response to "Hey" than "Hey." "…*Ho*," she added a second syllable just because she couldn't think of anything better at that particular moment. "Hey-*ho*, Tribb."

Hey-ho? Smooth move. Brilliant.

Courtney and Cricket threw a tiny ball of paper at Tribb's head from their prime spots. "Hey, Tribb!" They giggled.

Tribb flashed a BriteWhite smile at them.

"I've been looking all over for you!" Tribb said to Parker. "We should totally try and coordinize." He checked his popped collar. Beaver and Kirby followed.

Parker was so relieved. He was finally going to bring it up. All really *would* be well. Matin would be over and she could focus 100% on Fall Sosh. She could almost forget that her mom might move…

"Right. Yes! Coordinize!" Parker couldn't have agreed more. "So my dress is blue," she told him. "Kiki calls it *azul*."

"Your dress *is* azul," Kiki added. "*Pale* azul."

"But that's basically just a fancy word for blue." Parker fluttered her fingers around her neck where the dress came up to. "It has this really great neckline. And I've been thinking *absolutely no jewelry*." She laughed. "The corsage really says it all."

"Your *dress?*" Tribb asked. His voice was low, like a mallet hitting a big brass gong. "I meant the Ancient Egypt Living Museum project thing. I need to at least get a C."

"Virtual Humanities? The project thing?" Parker's heart dropped. Tribb had no plans at all to coordinate his tux with her dress. She didn't even know what time he was picking her up. "Sure," she said. "Living Museum."

"Sweet." Tribb nodded back to Parker. "You're the greatest, Park." He winked.

"Sure." Parker cleared her throat. "No probs."

"What color's your dress?" Kirby asked Plum. When he spoke, his cheeks turned red in patches that looked like the shape of Pennsylvania. "It's wicked sick, I bet."

Plum turned around and flashed Kirby the mini–evil eye (no serious injuries incurred). "Me no speakum guyanese,

Kirby," she notified him. "But it's lavender anyway, if you must know," she admitted. "With little black polka dots."

Mrs. Rouse sat down at the piano and the lights dimmed. Parker's brief social moment was immediately replaced with a feeling of dread. It was too late for Hotchkiss to do anything.

"OMGeeze!" Ikea grabbed Parker's arm. "He's here!" Ikea pointed to the back of the auditorium. Mr. Bentley was sitting at the end of the row. He hadn't taken off his overcoat and his limo driver was standing behind him. "He's supposed to be in court! *Please* say she's not going to show it, Parker," she pleaded. "She can't!"

Parker looked past Mr. Bentley and his driver at the silhouette of James sitting in the AV booth. McDweebs was back there with him, she could see. The familiar clip-clop of the Terminator's chic but sensible high heels approaching the podium was even more nerve splitting from the front row.

"No way Hotchkiss is going to show it," Parker said confidently, even though her dread had turned to panic. "No way." She crossed every finger she had as the room went dark.

Chapter 25

*F*ITZ ORION ONCE TOLD me 'I'm going to make a difference in the universe,'" Hotchkiss announced at the podium. "He was just a student at Wallingford Academy at the time." The Terminator's demonic buildup gave Parker a horrible, sinking feeling. "And Fitz Orion *did* make a difference in the universe after all."

Ikea turned around. Her father was still sitting there in the back.

"What is she talking about, Parker?" Ikea whispered, squirming.

"I can't tell," Parker said. "Something about the solar system, maybe?"

The soft music began on her command. Parker suddenly couldn't breathe. She felt like she was under water.

"And speaking of *different*..." Hotchkiss looked directly at Parker and raised her Genius Pen to her shiny black tablet.

The world is going to end. Right here, right now, Parker thought. With the touch of her stylus, the Terminator was finally going to annihilate all mankind. Or maybe it was just the Lylas who were going to be destroyed.

Hotchkiss pressed the pen lightly and the Super-Screen illuminated with the *Wallingford Academy Today* logo. Parker began to shake so hard she had to hold onto her armrests to keep from falling off her chair.

Ikea began to shake. Kiki's head dropped like a deadweight into her lap. Plum curled in her seat like one of those dolls that turns into a backpack.

Parker felt like the floor fell out from beneath her.

• • •

The show's opening song—Liam Davies's latest hit—blasted out through the finely tuned acoustics of the elegant Freeman Auditorium. It was the loudest thing anyone had ever heard at the school. Years ago a sudden explosion of sound like that would have sent hundreds of Wallys and teachers running for the old bomb shelter. Even Parker had to put her fingers in her ears as the bone-splitting grind ricocheted around the great rotunda, nearly shattering the grand chandelier.

Those who had not already passed out (like Mrs. Rouse, onto her piano keys) or become coma-toast (like Allegra Oliphant and a half dozen other Einsteins) or popped out a Hollywood Hair Bumpit (like Tinsley Reardon, onto Courtney Wallace's lap), were thrashed by flashes of silver, swirls of light and fog, and caboodles of Plum's DayGlo universe.

The set was downright sedate in real life compared to the way it came off on the stadium-sized Super-Screen. And James's filming—the "feeling of movement without the whole hand-held trap" and the "compression effect without all the old school distortion"—made the studio feel like a glimpse from a spaceship rather than what it was: a dark spare room in the basement of the school, a couple of cans of bright "door-hinge," some junkyard furniture and Plum's mother's spinning Pilates ball covered in mirror tiles. There weren't enough yellow slips in Death Breath's entire collection to even begin listing all the rules that'd been broken.

Parker wasn't sure if she'd ever start breathing again. She took her fingers out of her ears, opened her eyes and stared up at the screen.

"Hello, and welcome to Wallingford Academy Today! I'm your host, Parker Bell, and we're streaming to you from the studio here in the bowels of our dorky school, Wallingford Academy..."

Even before Parker finished delivering her opening line, the entire audience broke out in laughter. Parker cringed. The voices were unmistakable: Kirby, Courtney, Cosima, Tinsley, Laurel, Natalie, even Tribb. All laughing at her. She could even hear Barn Yard's cackling behind her.

There was nothing worse, Parker realized—no terrible disease, no dissected cow eyeball guts—*nothing* more gruesome and paralyzing than the feeling of the whole world laughing at you. Parker's insides felt like they had just melted onto the floor never to be gathered up again.

The footage cut away from Parker's public humiliation to the video clip of Graham Henry belching the Alma Mater beside the portrait of Miss Thistle in the foyer of the school. Only this *was* supposed to be funny—but not a single person in the room was laughing. (Except Graham Henry himself, of course.) In fact, the Freeman Auditorium was so painfully silent, it felt like the whole school had turned into one giant ice cube. Everyone's faces were stuck in a single position, like the entire room was playing a giant game of Freeze Tag.

Allegra Oliphant smirked from her spot down the row.

"Mind your own beachwax, Allegra!" Kiki snapped.

Parker had almost forgotten that Ikea's sharp fingernails were digging into her arm. She was glad her body was completely numb or else the ten tiny vice grips would have sent her screaming.

Please let the computer crash, Parker prayed. *Please let the electricity shut down in the whole school. Please let a random train come crashing through the stage. Please let an alien spaceship abduct me right now...* She glanced over at Ikea, whose hands were clasped in silent prayer, as well.

But the webcast just kept rolling.

Kiki had decided that she simply couldn't do the lunch menu *and* shop for dresses for Fall Sosh—so she just shopped for dresses (quel surprise). She did, however, do it in front of the camera, so they just edited her bit in.

> "We're here in the Langdon's designer frock salon picking out something *fabu* for Fall Sosh, the first truly major event of the season!"

Kiki sashayed through the fancy boutique. Kenneth came along while Kiki shopped because Kenneth always came along for things like this: haircuts, mani-pedis, Fake-n-Bakes. *Somebody* had to sprawl out on a grand divan (even when the cameras *weren't* rolling) and read magazines aloud. That somebody was Kenneth.

> "Now lace is evil. It truly is. You *think* it's going to be smashing, but really it's a horrendous material. It makes everyone look like a stuffed sausage. So this is why we won't even be *looking* at lace."

There were uncomfortable murmurs coming from the back of the eighth grade section. Parker assumed from the girls who were planning to wear lace. The audience's game of freeze tag continued. On screen, Keeks & Kenneth gabbed about dresses and shoes, gossiped about celebrities, and played "Who Wore It Better?" with the webcast audience. Kenneth showed the camera the pages of his magazine inviting everyone to submit their opinions online.

"Do you think I look fat?" Kiki asked Parker. "That side's my fat side I think."

"Who cares what you look like, Kiki? Our lives are over!" Parker hissed, unable to contain her hairy nip. "Who cares?!"

"You don't have to be such an insultosaurus, Park. What's the matter with you anyway?" Kiki slumped down into her seat. "And, I was just testing you, F-Y-I. The *other* side's my fat side!"

Ikea's hand was all clammy on Parker's.

"I can't believe this, Parker," Ikea said softly.

"I'm so sorry, Ike," Parker said. "I really didn't think she would show it." Together, in the giant ice cube that was the Freeman Auditorium, they continued to watch.

James had the idea of filming Ikea from just slightly below a normal level. It made her seem even larger than she would have on the Super-Screen. Her Afro alone looked as big as the moon. No one had ever seen Ikea like this before. There was a collective OMGasp in the auditorium.

"A friend of mine told me that everyone in this school knows me already, so I guess I don't have to introduce myself. But the *are* a few other people I'd like you to meet..."

165

Ikea (the one shivering in her seat, not the one stomping a suede boot on the screen) closed her eyes. Her sweater sleeves were pulled out away from her arms and twisted limply around her like she was in a straightjacket.

Parker didn't dare turn around and look at Ikea's father.

"For those of you who have *no clue* who these people are—and that's *most* of you—I'd like to introduce them. Because, uh, *hello*, they go to school with you! And, if the administration is listening (you know who you are), there *should be* thirty-nine point six more of them here. *At least.* So—if you know me, you should know them too: The few, the proud, the shockingly outnumbered: The fourteen underappreciated *students of color* at Wallingford Academy!"

The petrified, fidgety silence in the room was suddenly broken by Wallys' screams and whistles. Fourteen Wallys to be exact. The under-appreciated fourteen that were each about to have their moment of Super-Screen glory: Kiki had done their outfits, Plum had done makeup, Kenneth hair, and Parker had coordinated the complex location scouting and studio schedule that allowed for each of them to have their moment in front of James's camera at a location of his or her own choosing. Even with Advanced Geometry, it was one of the most complicated equations Parker had ever solved.

"Divya Venkataraghavan!"

McDweebs had cut away from the shot of Ikea standing

in the studio. Divya marched into the middle of the screen, did a Top Model turn, snapped in a *Z* like Kenneth had shown her, and smiled proudly, her silver braces gleaming in the light. She wore a formal *salwar kameez* embroidered with gold, and a traditional studded nose ring with a long chain attached. James had filmed her in the ornate foyer of her parent's home.

There were hushed whispers around the room. *Who was that? Did she go to this school? Do you know her? Do you?*

Divya was easily the most exotic and glamorous Wally nobody had ever seen.

"Brooks Jenkins the Third!"

Brooks wanted to be filmed in front of his father's Lamborghini Countach—a car, Brooks had boasted to Parker, he'd inherit when his father croaked.

"Ashanti Wiseman!"

Ikea introduced them all one by one.

"Lily Del Milagro Maldonado! Yu Chen! Diana Taylor!"

The once-silent audience worked into a frenzy as the fourteen students of color took their moment of glory. They chanted Ikea's name over and over again: "*I-kay-ya! I-kay-ya! I-kay-ya!*"

But the cheers only made the real Ikea squirm in her chair. Parker put her arm around her friend and turned around quickly to see what Mr. Bentley was doing. His seat was empty.

"He's gone," Parker told her gently. "You don't have to worry about him anymore."

"He's gone?" Ikea turned around. "My dad walked out?" She was outraged. The roar of the crowd nearly drowned her out. "He walked out on me?"

"I don't know that he walked out really..." Parker tried to sound sure.

"He did," Ikea murmured. "I'm such a total idiot!"

"You're not an idiot, Ikea." Plum reached out but Ikea yanked her hand away.

"You're the smartest girl I know," Kiki tried to console her.

Ikea held down her puffy ponytails and ran out of the auditorium crying.

Sometimes Parker could feel bad just *because*—like when something bad happens but deep down in your heart you know it's not that big of a deal. This wasn't *that* kind of "feel bad" for Parker—this was the kind that deep down in your heart made you feel terrible. Like you just broke something delicate that could never be fixed, not even with Crazy Glue. She sat paralyzed in her seat. She should have known better—she started out the year wanting to be a shining example for everyone and now she'd done the worst thing a person could do.

She'd let down her friends.

"This is all your fault, Parker," Kiki declared. "You said Hotchkiss would never show it."

Parker saw her face on the Super-Screen again. She braced herself for the end.

"This is Parker Bell signing off. Until next time—*Stay pretty*, Wallingford!!"

Parker didn't dare sneak a look back at Tribb as she ran out. She couldn't look at anyone.

Chapter 26

*I*KEA WASN'T BY THE old phone booths. She wasn't in any of the stalls in La Cachette. She wasn't in the studio or Tea & Wardrobe. Parker even used the Spy Feed to try and find her. Ikea wasn't anywhere in the school.

Kiki wasn't speaking to Parker, and Plum just decided she didn't want to get in the middle of the whole thing so she wasn't talking to anyone.

In other words, the Lylas no longer existed.

• • •

"Hey." Tribb swaggered up to Parker's locker at the end of the day. She didn't do the by-her-locker pose or try and think of something clever. She just looked up.

"Hey," she replied.

"That was sure a real…" Tribb tried to think of the right word, "…*webcast*."

"And I totally forgot about the bootleg recording," she said. "I'm sorry I…"

"Everybody's talking about the show," he interrupted. "I heard you guys already have fans everywhere."

"I bet." Parker already knew about their *fans*. She grabbed her French book from the shelf in her locker and shut the door.

"Oh, hey. I just remembered…" Tribb thought of one more thing in that way someone thinks of one-more-thing when that's really what they wanted to talk about in the first place. "I didn't want you to think that *you*…and *I*…like that whole Fall Sosh thing. *Us* and everything," Tribb said with a funny look on his face.

Parker wasn't sure what Tribb was getting at but she could pretty much guess.

"N*ooooo*." Parker faux-laughed at the mere thought. "Me and you?" *Pa-lease!* "That whole azul dress with the neckline thing? Just JKing," she said convincingly. "Totally," she added. "Fall Sosh! Not *at all*."

"Because I'm just, you know," he said, "doing my *thang*. Right?" That funny look still clung to Tribb's face like a popped bubble of Bazooka.

"Me too!" Parker agreed wholeheartedly. "My own *thang*."

The funny thing was, she should have felt terrible. But there was just so much *terrible* already hanging off of her, another backpack full of it didn't seem to make much of a difference. The weirdest part? The thing she thought about most was not getting the gardenia wrist corsage. She'd wanted the smell of it to swirl around her all that evening. She wanted to go to bed that night with the flower next to her on her pillow. A gardenia corsage, she thought, meant someone really great kind of loved her. Or *might* love her. Or might consider loving her someday.

"That's great." Tribb smiled. "Because I always want to be honest with you, Parker. I mean, we're friends, right?"

"Yeah," she said. "Absolutely."

"Sweet." Tribb nodded as he popped his collar and headed for the vestibule.

Parker looked up, halfway hoping that Tribb might turn around. That he might someday feel the same way about her that she did about him.

171

She didn't cry about it until she got into the bathroom.

• • •

Parker went to Wallingford Towne Centre and tried on three different colors of Lipglass at World of Beauty but she couldn't tell if any of them looked good on her.

Ikea would have known, she thought. Kiki too. And Plum.

She bagsied the comfy couch at La Coppa Coffee and tried to enjoy her half-caf venti mocha macchiato, but she couldn't. All of the fun of a mocha mach was drinking it with her friends. (She didn't even like coffee when she was by herself.) She tossed her full cup in the garbage and wandered over to the Orion store and tried out a few of the new gadgets. Fitz Orion (or actually *the holographic likeness* of Fitz Orion) was in the center of the store showing one of his newest creations, the Orion holoPod, a holographic music video player.

Customers were standing around the ghost-like image of Fitz, grabbing at the vision again and again like they might scoop up a piece of him and stuff it in their pockets. But they were all gathering up nothing—reaching out again and again for something that didn't exist.

Why do people do that? Parker wondered. Why do they keep thinking something will be there when it's not and never will be? Why do they keep reaching with their fingers as if this time might be different—as if this time something real might appear right there in their hand?

But Parker knew why. She knew that when you wanted something *so badly* you held out this endless bucket of hope. You believed in magic. You believed in wishes. You kept reaching out again and again, believing that someday you might open your palm and find something real in there.

Chapter 27

The five rules of Fall Sosh:

1. Tiny totes are in for evening.
2. Girls should not wear tuxedos, even in an ironic sense.
3. No line dancing.
4. No white, flaky deodorant.
5. Never dance alone.

*K*IKI CAREFULLY UNZIPPED THE blue canvas dress bag from Langdon's and let it drop to the closet floor in a puddle beneath her brand new frock. The material of the ankle-length gown was a luminous, pale eggshell duchesse, ever-so-slightly ruched along the side, with tiny Swarovski crystals and pearls sewn in a swirl pattern around the bodice. The saleswoman at Langdon's said it took three seamstresses more than a month to make it. Francesca Brandon, she'd said, had worn a similar one to the Emmys.

The dress was, in a word, *smashing*.

And Kiki *had* to have it. Her life depended on it. (At least it felt like it did at the time.) She'd used her jet-black Centurion Card to pay for it instead of her Langdon's house charge. It was a good thing because the black plastic had no limit.

Kiki unhooked the dress from its golden hanger, walked it carefully into the bedroom and laid it out on top of the lace coverlet of her princess bed. The layers of duchesse and tulle rustled as it all settled into place.

In her fuzzy slippers and PJs, she stood above the dress on the bed and ate all the marshmallows out of her box of Lucky Charms. She was careful not to drop any of the pink hearts, yellow moons, orange stars, or green clovers down on the silky material. She pictured herself wearing it—her soft updo with little tendrils hanging down, her delicate, radiant-cut solitaire necklace, her matching Duvelle shoes and handbag, her pale, pretty makeup.

Normally something like this would make Kiki so happy she'd be crawling out of her skin, counting down the seconds until she could zip it up along her back and ask Esmerelda to clasp the solitaire around her neck. Normally, she would've started the process already: getting the mani-pedi, soaking in the tub, texting Parker nonstop, posting shoe options on Facebook for everybody's vote, and doing the Birdie so hard that lifting off and flying like a helicopter over her house was not as improbable as it sounded.

Instead Kiki crawled back into her bed and hid underneath the covers. Her beautiful new dress laid in position on top of her as if she *and* the bed were wearing it.

She turned to one side and held her downy pillow close to her body. She took off her friendship ring and held it up to the light. *Friends Forever.*

Her life really didn't depend on a dress. Or a pair of shoes. Or a radiant-cut solitaire. Or a soft updo with little tendrils. Without the Lylas, the dress was just a heap of material sewn together by a bunch of little old Italian ladies. Hair was just hair. The necklace was just a rock on a chain.

Without her friends by her side, she felt deflated. Like a dress with no one in it.

• • •

Plum plucked her eyebrows and listened to music as she got ready. The Black Daphnes was an all-girl emo group. All they sang about was hating boyfriends, hating super-perky people, and hating bands who sold their songs to be used in car commercials. Listening to all that depression always made Plum feel pretty good. It was like somebody she didn't even know understood what it felt like to be her.

She dreamed that she and the Black Daphnes could hang out.

The sharp smells of her mother's cooking dinner wafted up from the kitchen downstairs. Plum wasn't going to eat a plate of cheese pierogi before the dance. Pierogi were good and everything, but Russian food was something you needed to eat when there was a lot of time to recover. Her mother's cooking, she thought, rebuilt the ozone layer one toot at a time.

Plum put the finishing touches of the black liner over her eyelashes with a small, sharp swoop up at the end, like a cat's eye. She waved her hands in front of them so they would dry all the way before she blinked (made *that* mistake before).

While her cat eyes finished drying, she pulled a photograph of the Lylas down from the corner of her corkboard: a picture of the four of them in third grade tobogganing down the big hill together in Shenley Park. Parker was first, Ikea second, Kiki third, and Plum was at the top. It was snowing and they were all bundled up. Their cheeks were pink. Hot chocolates were waiting for them when they got back home. This is the way they were supposed to be, Plum thought—the four of them stuck together like a train: the Little Engine That Always Could.

Plum tacked the photograph back onto her board. *The whole thing was just so stupid,* she thought. It was supposed to be the best year of their lives, and instead, it was Fall Sosh and they weren't even speaking.

Kiki, Plum imagined, was probably in her closet stresserizing, frantically yanking expensive shoes off shelves, eating all the marshmallows out of a jumbo cereal box, and driving Esmerelda bonkies trying to figure out which handbag made her look the least fat. It'd be a miracle if Keeks made it out of the house before Fall Sosh was over. Plum had to laugh a little when she thought about it.

And at this very moment, Plum imagined, Parker was doing her mascara one eyelash at a time, fluffing bronzer onto every visible part of her body, and practicing kissy face with Tribb in front of her mirror. Parker might have been upset about how everything with the webcast had turned out, but at least she wasn't going to the dance alone. Parker always landed on her feet.

And *Ikea*—Plum thought—Ikea was just being confused. She couldn't be exactly what her father wanted her to be, but maybe that wasn't so bad. If every girl spent her life trying to be what her father wanted her to be the whole world would be filled with Yale lawyers, nuns, people who didn't kiss until they were married, and first woman presidents. There were a few girls on the planet who needed to do something other than those things. Maybe Ikea was one of them.

She wanted to tell Ikea that. She wanted to help Parker with her mascara and her terminal overuse of mineral bronzer. She wanted to assure Kiki that *both* sides were her good side. And she sort of wanted to tell them that she secretly *liked* Kirby Vanderbilt even though his one front tooth was bigger than the other and his neck was kind of skinny.

Plum lifted her new bra out of the box from American Coquette. It was the Fantasia II, a new and improved version of the original Fantasia. It was the strapless model with Featherlift and Volumizer Inserts.

She held it up to her body and looked in the mirror. She was finally developing, she thought. Sort of. Slightly. Maybe-possibly. Well, if nothing else, her bra was developing. At least it was something.

• • •

Parker put the blow dryer on its coolest setting and aimed it at her eyelashes. She'd layered them lightly with two coats of mascara, wiggling the wand on the uppers and the lowers like Plum had once shown her. She wanted them to dry completely before she blinked (made *that* mistake before). She wanted them to look as good as when Plum did them.

She got dressed faster than usual: underwear, dress, shoes, handbag, yada yada. It was easy to do things quickly when you didn't care that much (which she didn't). Care much felt like some emotion from the past. Definitely not meant for tonight. She'd spent so many hours dreaming about this moment and now it was here. And it sucked.

She didn't even look in the mirror at the pale azul dress with the really great neckline. She decided to go absolutely-no-jewelry even though she knew the corsage wasn't coming. *Jewelry was for celebrating.*

Completely ready and with nearly an hour to kill, Parker sat at her desk and opened her computer. She was tempted to go to the *Wallingford Academy Today* website and look at the show again. *Tempted*—like you're tempted to scratch at a scab on your knee or bite off a hangnail.

Instead she opened Facebook, a thing she hadn't done in weeks. Her status was so outdated it wasn't even funny. She couldn't bear to read the comments on her wall or look at her honesty box or check out any of the graffiti anyone had done for her. And the only Friend request still pending was her mother. And that was still pretty icky.

She scrolled to the section where you find people you know. For some reason she typed:

James Hunter

Hundreds of James Hunters came up. She skimmed through the first three-hundred or so, sure that the next page would be the one. There was a bald James Hunter from Minneapolis. A bunch from England. One from New Zealand. And there were tons of James Hunters with no profile pictures—but people with no pictures didn't really count. She hoped the James Hunter she was looking for wasn't one of them. He kind of counted. Even if he wasn't on FB.

She typed in Cricket Von Wielding's name. There weren't too many Crickets, and Von Wielding pretty much narrowed it down to one.

Despite the invitation, Parker still wasn't her Friend, but Cricket didn't seem to need the help—she had five-hundred-and-eighty-two Friends. One hundred and eighty-four more than Parker. Many of the faces were familiar: the Crickettes. Once *her* Friends.

The Lylas and the populadder. Gone for good.

Parker shut down her computer. It was time to get the worst night of her life over with.

• • •

Ikea's mother, Sunday, poked her head into Ikea's bedroom. Ikea was nearly finished getting ready—she just had to wrap the top part of her dress on and slip into the traditional sandals that went with it. Sunday came in and helped her with the knot.

"In Benin," Sunday said, "this is a dress you might wear to a wedding. A very *elegant* lady would wear it." She tucked a bit of material up under the knot until it was secure. "Your grandmother would not have known such a beautiful thing might be worn by her grandchild." She smiled. Ikea's mother's face was impossibly beautiful, even without makeup. "She would be very proud of you."

Ikea looked in the mirror and managed a sad grin. She liked thinking about her grandmother even though she'd died long before Ikea was even born.

Sunday walked over and stood behind her daughter. "And I know how hard this is for you to believe," she said, "but your father is *very* proud of you." She rested her hands on Ikea's shoulders. "He just doesn't always know how to say the words. That doesn't mean he doesn't feel them."

Ikea looked closely at their two faces in the mirror. She tried to imagine her grandmother's face there too. And her great grandmother's—until all her ancestors' faces filled the mirror.

• • •

"I guess I'm ready." Parker walked into her mother's room. She had to lift up the hem of her dress to avoid stepping on it.

"*Parker!*" Ellen Bell was standing by her closet, probably

alphabetizing her clothes by designer and starting a card catalog for the whole collection. Ellen nearly dropped the sweater she was folding. "*Wow!* Sweetheart..."

"What?" Parker turned around because it seemed like her mom was talking to someone else.

"You look *absolutely* stunning," she said. "You take my breath away."

"I don't feel absolutely stunning," Parker replied. "I feel like a lump of *bleh* wearing a fancy dress."

"Well, you wouldn't know to look at you."

Ellen walked close to her daughter and put her arms around her. In heels, Parker was almost the same height.

Parker rested her head on her mother's shoulder. She felt like crying but she'd spent so long doing her eyelashes, she just sort of snortled, breaking a two-year-old rule: *Never snortle in public.* Her mother stroked her hair but was careful not to mess up anything. (That's kind of the way mothers were. They messed up other stuff, but Hair & Makeup was rarely one of them.)

"Cricket Von Wielding has about a million Friends," Parker said sadly. "And I have exactly *none*." She tried to use the moment to wriggle away but her mother held on.

"It's not always about a number." Ellen lifted Parker's face and looked her in the eye. "You know what I mean?"

Parker nodded. She knew what her mother meant but it didn't make her feel any better. She just wanted everything to be over with already.

"I got a call from the real estate agent today..." Ellen said into Parker's ear.

"Fox Chapel will be okay, Mom," Parker reassured her mother. "I can make new friends."

"Someone from Orion Computers called and asked about shooting a television commercial here at the house for a new product called a holoPod," Ellen said. "It's only for two days, but you can't believe how much they pay. It's enough money to get us through Christmas! Maybe longer if I pick up a small client." Ellen exhaled when the last few words came out. "So you can stay at school!" She wrapped her arms tightly around Parker. "Isn't that amazing news?"

Parker closed her eyes. She wasn't sure what to think about it—leaving was beginning to feel like the best thing to do.

"I've got just the thing for you…" Ellen abruptly ended the Mom-hug-moment and ran into her bathroom. She opened her vanity and pulled out a cut-crystal bottle with a black tassel dangling from its stopper. The bottle was tiny but the golden liquid was potent as Ellen dabbed a drop from the glass stopper on either side of Parker's neck.

"There," Ellen said when she was done. "Gardenia." She smiled. "*That's* what you needed."

Chapter 28

*I*T HAD BEEN SIMPLE to turn Wallingford Academy into a celebration of "A Harvest Moon," the theme of this year's Fall Social. Hotchkiss just had to push a button on her Tablet and the upper Super-Screens were filled with dark, starry skies. The wind rustled through the trees on the lower ones. Shadows of clouds seemed to pass overhead. If you looked at it all long enough, you could feel the chill of the autumn night. Or maybe that was some new special effect. Knowing Fitz Orion, he'd probably figured out how to make the *actual* wind blow.

Parker held up the hem of her dress and walked quickly into La Cachette. She couldn't imagine touching up her lipstick anywhere else. Or maybe she just wasn't ready to go into the ballroom. Maybe she could just hide out in La Cachette all night.

There was the sound of giggling behind two of the three stalls. Parker half-hoped it would be the Lylas, but it was just Cosima and Suzanne.

"Hi, Parker!" They washed their hands and dried them with one of the embroidered linen cloths folded in a stack beside the sink. "OMGorgies!" they said. "We're loving the dress!"

"Yours are even nicer," Parker managed. "Très gorgies."

Their dresses *were* nice. Cosima's was periwinkle satin with a simple empire waist. It was one of the "need-need" dresses at Langdon's that Kiki had tried on for her lunch menu segment,

Parker remembered. Suzanne's dress looked familiar too—another of Kiki's rejects.

"You've been, like, *invisibla* since Matin!" Suzanne said.

"*Everyone's* talking about it," Cosima added.

"It's all the goss!" Cosima giggled and checked her hair in the mirror. Suzanne started laughing too.

"OMGasp for air, Coz!" Suzanne said to Cosima through her fits of laughter. "That thing you said before...*that thing* was soooo funny, I'm in *hysterica!*"

"I know, right?!" Cosima nearly choked on chuckles.

Parker knew what Suzanne meant. It's not like she'd never done that trick before. It was pretty *obvy* what they were laughing about.

"Bye*hahaha*, Parker!" They were both nearly ROFL when they walked out of La Cachette.

Parker's hands were shaking when she reached into her tiny tote and pulled out her lipstick. *Tiny totes were in for evening.* She'd followed the Rule. The Rules felt like all she had left of the Lylas. She ran a layer of the frosty pink gloss over her lips and tried to think of some reasons why she shouldn't just stay in La Cachette all night.

"Hi, Parker."

Ikea walked out of the third bathroom stall. She'd been so quiet (or Coz and Suzanne had been so loud) that Parker hadn't heard her in there. The colors of Ikea's dress were as vivid as a rainforest. Parker understood what her mother had meant about "taking your breath away." Or maybe she was just so happy to see Ikea, she couldn't use her lungs.

"It's really hard to go to the bathroom in this thing," Ikea said, yanking at the bright material layered around her waist.

"You look really great, Ike," Parker said. "Like you could be a historical figure or something." The two of them stood still and far apart, as if inching any closer might cause one of them to suddenly disappear.

"You look even better, Park," Ikea said. "Your mascara came out really well."

"You think?" Parker turned and checked her lashes in the mirror. "I did that little trick-thingie Plum showed me."

"I'm sorry I didn't reply to your Facebook pokes," Ikea said. "Or your Skype pings. Or the texts. Or the *actual note* you left in the mailbox."

"Yeah," Parker laughed, "I decided to go primitive."

"I just *couldn't*, Park..." Ikea said regretfully. "My dad's been at the office all day and I was barely able to get out of bed." She looked down. "I just wish he'd go away forever so I'd never have to see him again."

"You don't mean that." Parker walked over and held Ikea's hand.

"I guess not," Ikea admitted.

"You know, I'm really, r*eeea*lly sorry," Parker told her. She tried to find better words to say but it wasn't like she'd practiced this in the mirror. "I feel like I haven't been myself since this whole thing started. I feel like I let the Lylas down—like I let *you* down."

"You don't have to be sorry, Parker," Ikea said. "I was thinking about it and I decided I'm proud of what I did. I was so busy worrying that I was going to fail at something that I never took any risks. But that's not the kind of person I want to be." She looked at herself in the mirror. "And you helped me see that."

Parker smiled. She was proud of Ikea too—it was the boldest

thing anyone she knew had ever done. "I actually thought it was really pretty cool." She laughed. "I heard Divya had like *eight* guys ask her to Fall Sosh!"

"Really?!" Ikea seemed excited for the first time since before Matin. "Where's Tribb?" she asked. "I bet he looks hawt in a tux!"

"…Alterations completely messed this up!" Kiki burst through the door with Plum following behind her. Kiki looked as if she'd just marched offstage of a couture production of Cinderella. The voluminous layers of her dress took up most of the floor of La Cachette. "The seams are in all the wrong places!" She fiddled with her zipper in the mirror. "I can't even *breathe,* it's so tight."

Parker and Ikea just stood there staring. Kiki had been known to overdress upon occasion, but she'd truly outdone herself. Neither of them could speak.

"What?" Kiki asked, looking down at a dozen yards of hand-sewn eggshell duchesse and enough Swarovski crystals to hang a chandelier. "I say if you're going to fall off the populadder completely, you might as well be a ledge at it. Right?" She fluffed up her skirt. "And you guys look ferosh, BTDubs." She turned around to fix her hair in the mirror. "You two all made up? Because I'm truly not loving the whole no-one's-talking sitch…" Kiki didn't miss a beat. "For one, it's completely daft, and for two, Esmerelda is having about ten nip fits a day because I have no one else to whinge to. *OMGroan,* this dress is so t*iiii*ght." She wiggled then turned to the side and sucked in her stomach.

Kiki tried to look innocent but everyone in the room knew that it wasn't the dress that had changed sizes. "All I ate today were some Lucky Charms," she swore.

"Well, you *do* look magically delicious," Parker admired.

"*Charming*, I would say," Ikea added.

"LOL." Kiki tried to exhale just a tiny bit at a time. "Hey… where's Tribb?"

"I was *so* hoping you guys would be here…" Plum had a puffy winter coat wrapped around her lavender dress with matching All-Stars high tops. Even the streak in her hair was dyed lavender. As soon as the door shut behind her, she whipped open her coat to reveal a bust the size of Barbie's.

Kiki gasped. "Is that the *Fantasia II*?!"

"What do you think?" Plum lifted the foam rack up a little and adjusted her dress. She admired herself in the mirror. "Good, right?"

"Really natural," Parker said quickly.

"Super-native," Ikea observed.

"As fab as it gets," Kiki added. (Lying to each other was definitely against the Rules, but flattery wasn't. *Flattery was always in.*)

"Like you think someone…*Kirby,* for an example…" Plum asked, "would think I looked completely normal?" She took off her puffy coat and shoved it into a little hiding place under the sink.

"Kirby *Vanderbilt?*" Kiki asked (the question nearly popped her zipper).

"You look unbelievably great," Parker told her. "Kirby's going to die when he sees you, Plum."

"Good," Plum said. Parker wrapped her arm around Plum's waist and they all took each other by the hand. "Oh yeah… where's Tribb?" Plum remembered as she pushed open the door of La Cachette.

186

"Not coming," Parker said. "At least not with me."

"Oh." Plum managed a half-a-smile. "Got it."

Parker didn't have to say anything else to her friends and that was just fine by her. The Lylas knew exactly how she felt—even without any more words.

Chapter 29

$\mathcal{P}$ARKER WALKED FIRST DOWN the hallway toward the Doris Duke Ballroom on the top floor of the school— Kiki second, Plum third, and Ikea last. Now that the Lylas were back together (had they ever really been apart?) she didn't care who would be laughing at them at the dance. When you had the Lylas you could get through anything.

Even tonight.

The images of the night sky surrounded the Lylas as they walked, making it feel like they were making their way down a starlit road to a fancy party. The four of them had spent so much time in La Cachette that Fall Sosh was already in full swing. The music piped through the halls. They were almost an hour late. *Maybe,* just maybe, Parker hoped, they could sneak in and head for the back, without anyone really noticing.

Parker felt her heart beating hard beneath her dress. The heat of her skin made her mother's perfume seem like a bouquet of gardenias surrounding her face. She didn't feel nervous to face Tribb or Courtney or Cricket or even Ms. Hotchkiss, she felt, *what was the word…*strong.

The Lylas joined hands as Parker pushed the door open to the Doris Duke Ballroom.

The music was loud enough that Parker could feel the vibration through her shoes. She had to use her Upper Case Voice to be heard by the rest of them. "LET'S HEAD TO THE BACK!" she shouted. She added the universal symbol for "head to the back" (finger roll, finger roll, point, head nod) and they all followed.

Curtains billowed down in front of the tall windows and landed in satiny puddles on the floor. Gold tassels the size of pillows held them into place. The glass doors that led to the balcony outside were flung open and heaters over the exits kept the room from getting cold. Thousands of lanterns hung over their heads, or maybe it was just the illusion of lanterns. In this school, it was impossible to tell.

The Doris Duke Ballroom was packed with Wallys. Most were dancing and the rest were standing tightly against the walls kind of wiggling—like they wanted to dance but the centrifugal force of the room was too great to release them.

"There's Divya!" Plum said as she spotted Ikea's friend dancing with Duncan Middlestat, now a full-fledged upper tier Wally.

"She cut her hair!" Ikea yelled as the four of them tried to cram into the furthest away corner. "It's all layer-y!"

"Kenneth and I updated her profile," Kiki explained.

"Chic City!" Plum declared.

"We're loving it!" Ikea said.

Parker saw James out of the corner of her eye. He was alone in the AV booth. He hadn't dressed up for Fall Sosh the way most people might dress up (for example…Kiki), but he had brushed his hair and he wore a fitted cashmere sweater, instead of his usual baggy sweatshirt, over his black jeans. He looked nice, Parker thought. Should she say hello? She could see James turn his head toward her. Parker put her hand up to wave even though she knew it was too dark for him to see her.

"Danger, Danger, ex-EGB, nine o'clock." Kiki pointed to Tribb. He was wearing a white tuxedo jacket and dancing in between Courtney and Cricket (also wearing two of Kiki's "need-need" rejects). The three of them were violating at least one of the rules in the Wallingford Handbook: *Students of the opposite sex must stay at least eight inches away from each other at all school-sponsored galas,* and at least one of the Lylas's: *Never do the Sandwich-Dance. Not even as a joke.*

"He's not really my ex-EGB," Parker clarified over the music. "He's just hangin' right now. Doing his own thang." She smiled with conviction despite the raised eyebrows from the group. "He is…" The "he *is*…" came out not only unconvincing but also embarrassingly loud because the music had suddenly stopped.

Hotchkiss was standing on the stage in front of the microphone. She'd whipped up the lights just a notch with her pen. She was wearing what you'd expect the Terminator to wear to an event like this: a suspiciously normal black dress, a beady string of pearls, and chic but sensible high heels.

"We've been waiting for you ladies." Hotchkiss's voice boomed into the microphone. Her words echoed loudly in the giant ballroom.

"*Us?*" Plum whispered to Parker.

Every Wally had stopped dancing and turned around to the Lylas. Their whispers were like bees buzzing around them. Parker saw Cricket and Courtney giggling. Tribb bent his head down to Courtney, smiled and nodded. Kiki fluffed out the layers of crinoline under her dress (staying true to the new Rule that going down in flames should be done in style).

"Yes *you*, Miss Petrovsky!" Hotchkiss answered from all the way up on the stage (proving her super-stealth auditory powers yet again). "…And Miss Allen, Miss Bell, and Miss Bentley." She smiled a Grinchy smile.

Parker stiffened.

Mr. Bentley had just snuck in the back door to the ballroom. Plum and Kiki had seen him too, but Ikea's eyes never left the stage. No way were any of them going to point him out.

"Or more *specifically*," Hotchkiss enunciated, "we have a *special guest* who's been waiting for you." She nodded to James in the AV room.

Bad sign: Hotchkiss nodding to James could never lead to anything good.

Parker gulped as the lights dimmed again and what looked like a long sprinkler head descended from the center of the ballroom.

Death by sprinkler. It was possible. She'd seen the movie.

A tiny burst of electricity sprinkled out from the spigot like bright fireworks. Almost everyone in the room OMGasped. But the long electrostatic fingers spread out and around like a globe and joined the floor below. It was then that a holographic image of Fitz Orion appeared in the center of the room. He was smiling, wearing a red kimono and sitting on the floor of a Japanese-style room. A woman was kneeling beside him and serving him a small bowl of frothy green tea.

If he hadn't been projected about ten times larger than a real person, Fitz would have looked like he was right there. Parker remembered the customers in the Orion store desperately reaching out for scoops of him to put in their pockets. She wondered if this was live or prerecorded like it had been in the store.

"*Ohayou gozaimasu!*" The image spoke. "Good morning,

Wallingford Academy!" The image laughed. "…At least it's morning here." This wasn't prerecorded—this was happening right now, right here, somewhere else in the world. The infamous Fitz Orion was in the room.

Hotchkiss giggled. She hid her face behind her hand. The Wallys stood frozen in their fancy party clothes, stunned that the mega-billionaire was sitting there right in front of them (well, an enormous holographic likeness of the mega-billionaire anyway). Parker didn't know what was more shocking: Hotchkiss's sudden girlish transformation or the spectacular apparition before her.

"That's Fitz Orion!" Ikea grabbed Parker's arm. It's what everyone in the ballroom was saying.

Fitz sipped his bowl of tea and grinned. He was either about to say something monumental or take another sip of tea; it was impossible to guess.

"I'm going to tell you something you don't know," Fitz proclaimed. "Something I wouldn't have believed in a *million* years when I was your age." He brought his face nose-close in to his camera and whispered, "*Life. Is. Short*, my friends," he said. "It's gone in the blink of an eye. And in the grand scheme of things, in this vast cosmos that surrounds us, our puny little lives mean nothing." Fitz laughed so hard he had to put his tea down to keep from spilling it.

It didn't seem so incredibly funny to Parker but maybe there was some billionaire inside joke she was missing.

"So this past summer," Fitz continued, "Ms. Hotchkiss and I got to talking." Hotchkiss nodded as he spoke. Parker got the feeling she would have nodded at anything Fitz Orion had to say. "And we said: 'Why do we all have to be so terrified all the time?' Isn't that right, Ms. Hotchkiss?"

"Terrified. Yes. That's what we said." Hotchkiss responded although it wasn't clear that Fitz could hear her.

"…We're *terrified* of what people think of us," Fitz continued. "What our *friends* think of us. What our *parents* think of us. What *people we don't even know* think of us!" he said. "We spend so much time being terrified of everyone and everything that we hardly have a voice in this world." He took a steaming towel from the woman and pressed it to his face.

Every Wally in the room stayed silent until Fitz peeled the warm towel away and was ready to speak again.

"So we thought that *Wallingford Academy Today* could be that voice!" He opened his arms as wide as they would go. "Projected out into the cosmos! Not mine…not Ms. Hotchkiss's. *Your* voice!" His finger pointed so far outward Parker instinctively jumped back. "And…" He searched for something on the table in front of him. "As of about three minutes ago…" He found what he was looking for, a strange hand-held device—it looked like the one Parker had seen at the store: the Orion holoPod.

Fitz turned on the device. The *Wallingford Academy Today* website homepage began whirling around in front of him until it settled in a spot that everyone could see. "*Wallingford Academy Today* has nine-thousand, three-hundred and ninety-nine subscribers!" He read the numbers at the bottom of the page. "Heck, Kiki and Kenneth got over six-thousand responses to 'Who Wore It Better'!" Fitz leaned in to the camera again. "It was *Eliza*," he said. "Pretty obvy." He winked.

Kiki's Birdie couldn't be contained any longer. Even Kenneth nearly took off.

Parker's head spun. She hadn't checked the stats on the webcast since the beginning of the year when Arthur was the only subscriber. *Nine thousand?* She felt Ikea's fingers meet hers, and Plum's too.

"Subscribers from all over the planet," Fitz said. "There's even a girl here from Christmas Island!" He laughed. "That adds a *festive* touch."

"I told you," Kiki whispered.

"And this is just the beginning! This is *your* voice, Wallingford Academy!" Fitz declared. "So speak loud. Be fearless. The world is listening." The woman came back into view with a small bowl of rice. "Sayonara for now, my friends."

Fitz Orion reached forward and flipped a switch. In an instant, he was gone.

For what seemed like minutes, no one blinked or even breathed. Tribb Reese was the first Wally to start cheering. "Yeah!!" Tribb screamed, both arms high in the air. From Tribb it spread outward until everyone was sounding off.

Parker closed her eyes and listened to the applause. She imagined herself being lifted up and up and up. It would have been the most perfect moment of her life except that as she felt herself floating above the room, she realized that nothing was up there but the air and the clouds and the drop crystal pendants of the chandelier in the Doris Duke Ballroom.

There was nothing at all up there.

She felt the arms of her friends wrap around her and together they made their way through the crowd and up to the stage. The cheers continued as James joined them and McDweebs too. She stood there with the Lylas looking out at the audience of cheering Wallys and she felt complete—not because Fitz Orion had given their crazy webcast his blessing or because she had nine-thousand new Friends or even because she was wearing the perfect dress—but because she knew she was just fine without any of those things.

"If you've been wondering why I chose you for the webcast," Hotchkiss leaned in to Parker. "I didn't." She nodded toward the center of the room where Fitz had been. "*He* did."

Parker looked at the space where Fitz Orion had been, the founder of Orion computers, the genius everyone in the world wanted a piece of—and she wondered. Why would Fitz Orion have chosen *her?*

It was not a question she'd be able to answer tonight.

Chapter 30

APITAL O! CAPITAL M! CAPITAL G!" Suzanne and Tinsley, Cosima and Emily, Natalie and Laurel, and all of Parker's ex-best friends gathered around her. The only ones noticeably absent were Cricket and Courtney. They were over at the drinks table, Parker could see, reapplying Lipglass.

"We knew you were really onto something!" Natalie said.

"Fabulastic!"

"Way hysterica!"

"Beyond way!"

"And like, we're all famous now...I mean, *the school* is famous, which sort of means we all are too by default."

"Totally."

"I can't even belie*eee*ve it."

Parker hugged each of them and took their compliments. It was a funny combination of exciting and silly. It felt like they had all just been laughing at her just minutes before—Parker realized she couldn't take any of it too seriously. She looked over their heads for someone else.

"Those dresses look familiar, Keeks?" Kenneth asked Kiki loudly.

"They look like need-need dresses to me, Kenneth." Kiki grinned. Even her rejects were ledge.

"And she snaps her fingers in a *Z* formation!" Kenneth

congratulated Kiki with their now world famous sign-off. Kiki didn't return the gesture for fear of her zipper splitting. She just kept taking little breaths, hoping enough oxygen would eventually make its way in.

McDweebs walked up to them in a perfectly tailored tuxedo. His hair was freshly cut and styled. Very a la mo. Shocking, really. Parker had to give him his due: He looked more like a secret agent than a dweeb.

"Is that *you*, McDweebs?" Kiki was stupified—she'd know that tux anywhere. Diavolo for Men.

"It is," he said tugging on his bow tie. Had they not already gotten married in second grade, they could have tonight—they were both dressed for the occasion.

"Are you stalking me again?" Kiki asked.

"Nope," he said coolly. "I was just saying hello. *Hello*."

With that, McDweebs slid a hand in his pocket, turned around and began to walk away.

"McDweebs!" Kiki called out. "*Leonard...*or whatever."

"Yes?" He stopped and looked back.

"You look nice tonight," she said. "I mean in not too much of a completely dweebish kind of way," she added.

"Thanks. You too, Kiki." He smiled. "In fact, you look quite beautiful," he said as he walked away.

Kiki was left standing there. She watched as McDweebs walked out of the Doris Duke Ballroom.

"Hmm," she said aloud. Parker arched an eyebrow at her. Kiki just left it at that.

Out of the corner of her eye, Parker spotted Ikea—she'd finally got up the courage to walk up to her father. In her traditional dress, she was as impressive a figure as he was. Parker inched closer to eavesdrop. Not exactly breaking a rule…but she couldn't afford to miss this.

"Are you here on official business or something?" Ikea asked.

"I heard from *someone* that there might be a reason I should stop by." Mr. Bentley smiled and tried to do something with his hands. "I had to leave for court yesterday before I was able to critique your show…" he said uncomfortably.

"I know," Ikea said. "I remember."

"But I just wanted to say…" He cleared his throat. "I thought I'd say…"

"You wanted to say?" Ikea waited.

"I wanted to say that was a fine job!" He put a hand on her shoulder and patted it. "Attaboy!"

Ikea beamed. Parker had to beam, too. "Attaboy" might not have been the perfect way to put it, but it was the best he could do—and it was all Ikea needed.

• • •

As the congrats continued, Parker finally spotted James outside on the balcony. He'd put on a warm corduroy coat and was standing by himself. She could see the steam rising from his breath.

"The A League!" Tribb Reese startled her. He wrapped his arm around her waist like he might lift her in the air like a ballerina. Tribb raised an eyebrow and sort of *turned* to the side while still looking forward. If Parker wasn't mistaken, it looked like he might have been posing. Maybe he'd even practiced the move in front of the mirror. "So what do you think anyway?"

"About what?" she asked. *About being her EGB? About life? About Virtual Humanities?*

"About my future in television!" Tribb said. He was so excited he was out of breath. "Me? It? Us? You think?"

"What?" she asked. "I mean, sure. Completely. Yeah." Parker wasn't clear about what she was agreeing with but her answer put a smile on his face. He actually *did* lift her up in the air.

"Sweet!" Tribb said as he put her back down safely. He went to pop his collar but then remembered he was wearing the tuxedo jacket. "So me and the guys are going to Towne Centre for gelato after," he said. "Wanna come along?"

Parker had to stand on her tippy-toes to see if James was still out there.

"Uhh…" Parker wasn't quite sure how to answer. She looked at Tribb and his cute, happy face and smiled. He was really kind of sweet when he wasn't so busy being Tribb Reese, the soccer star. "I can't," she said. "Not tonight."

"That's okay. The limo was pretty full anyway." Tribb sounded like he didn't care either way. "Maybe some other time."

"Sure," Parker said as she walked toward the balcony. "Some other time."

• • •

It was cool outside and the moon was clear. No Super-Screen could ever really recreate that. Not even Fitz Orion had that much magic.

James was leaning against the ledge looking out at the sky. He didn't have his camera with him. It was the first time she'd seen him without it.

"Hi," Parker said.

"Hi." James said back. "You look really nice tonight," he

said. "That's a pretty dress." His eyes moved right to left, trying to talk to all of her at once.

"Thanks." Parker wrapped her arms around herself. Her teeth were chattering but she wasn't really cold. "You too. I really like your sweater." Complimenting the other person's new thing was a Rule but that's not why she said it. She didn't feel like she needed to follow any rules around James. She just spoke…the truth.

"Pretty crazy about the webcast, right?" Parker asked.

"Yeah," he said. "Pretty crazy."

It didn't matter what was on Parker's EGB list. Sitting next to James felt right. That was the only thing she needed to know about anything.

"You don't have your camera," she noted.

He held up his empty hands to her. She liked what they looked like with nothing in them. "Nope," he said. "Didn't feel like bringing it tonight."

James settled into his spot and looked up at the sky. She sat next to him and looked up. Her fingers were so close to his that it felt like a jolt of electricity was running between them. She wanted to rest her head on his shoulder or move close enough to him that his coat would fit around her too. But she didn't want to ruin it—she just wanted to breathe and soak it all in.

"Sometimes it's better without the camera," James told her. "You just close your eyes and remember the stuff you want to." He reached his hand closer and linked his pinky around hers.

She closed her eyes so she'd remember this exactly the way it was—the moon rising over the trees, the stars filling the sky…

Chapter 31

THE LYLAS WAITED OUT front on the stairs for their rides. The air was chilly and their dresses were now hidden under warm parkas, flannel-lined trench coats—or, in Kiki's case, a silver and black chinchilla. Cars and limousines lined up in the turnabout and Wallys poured out of the school. Divya came out laughing and holding Jake Emerson's hand.

"Bye you guys!" Divya said as she shut the door of her limo. She rolled down the window before she left. "This was the best night of my life!"

Ikea waved and made her fingers into the shape of a heart. Divya's ear-to-ear smile wasn't something Ikea could put on her college application or mention to the admissions committee, but it still was probably one of the most important things Ikea had ever done.

Tribb and Cricket came out, followed by Courtney and Tinsley and the guys from the team. They piled into the stretch Hummer in the turnabout.

"We're headed for gelato," Kirby yelled to Plum. "You wanna come?"

"I don't do Hummers," Plum said. "I have gas mileage issues." Kirby looked disappointed. "But I don't mind riding bikes," Plum added. "If you want to do that sometime."

"Sweet," he said as he shut the door.

Courtney's head popped up through the sunroof of the car. She was singing at the top of her lungs until Tinsley reached up and pulled her back down as the long car pulled away.

Allegra Oliphant's father was waiting in the long line of cars. Allegra walked out to meet him. She turned back to Parker.

"I guess congratulations are in order...but I personally can't endorse it," Allegra snipped.

"So then why don't you join the staff?" Parker asked. She wasn't just being a champion of the under-popular—she thought after those years of preparing for it, Allegra might actually have something important to say.

"Me?" Allegra asked as if it was the most unexpected thing she'd ever heard.

"Yeah," Parker said. "Why not?"

"I *do* have this eight-ring binder of ideas!" Allegra told her. "They're all alphabetized and categorized by relevance!"

"Oh great," Kiki griped. "*Eight*-ring? Fantabulous."

Allegra skipped out to her father's car. And if Parker wasn't mistaken, she was doing the Birdie all the way.

Kiki unstrapped her high heels and wiggled her toes. Parker's shoes were already off and her feet were freezing cold. Ikea lined up her sandals and crossed a foot over Parker's. Plum's lavender high tops fit right in beside them.

"What do you think we should do for the next show?" Ikea asked.

"I dunno..." Parker wasn't sure about what the future would bring. And that's just the way it was supposed to be. "We'll think of something."

The Aristobrats Essential Guide to Terms, Abbreviations, and Otherwise Completely Made-Up Words

Academy Awards acceptance pose   Hand on hip, other hand almost touching face. *Surprised! Flattered! Gracious!* Used in the event of, but not exclusive to, the winning of the award itself.

Aristobrats   What non-Aristobrats call the elite group of second, third, or even fourth generation Wallingford Academy students behind their backs.

Axe deodorant   1. What boys use instead of soap. **2.** That funny smell in the auditorium.

backblogged   The state of being behind on updating one's Facebook profile, often accompanied by a multitude of unread Friend requests, group invitations, fan suggestions, and photo tags. See *Facebook limbo.*

bagsy   **1.** To bag. **2.** To claim as by virtue of a right; *e.g., We bagsied the purple couch at La Coppa Coffee.*

the Birdie   The flapping of the hands by the shoulders so fast that you look like you might take off. Usually followed by a single excited squeal. Involuntary reflex.

blucher mocs   L.L. Bean four-eyelet moccasin (saddle brown), the foundation of the Aristobrat school uniform. Worn to old-shoe perfection. Infinitely preferable to the Top-Sider. Refer to *Essential Guide to "So Over."* The shoe for which the phrase "Don't drag your shoes, ladies" was created.

BTdubs   BTW, only better.

Carbo Footprint   A measure of the amount of carbohydrates (i.e., frosted brown sugar cinnamon Pop Tarts) utilized by a person, place, or organization at a given time.

def   *Definitely,* when constrained on time to say entire word.

distressing   So hawt it's painful. See *EGB.*

EGB   Eighth Grade Boyfriend. Possibly the most significant person in a person's life. Candidates have been evaluated for at least one year prior and agreed upon by at least two impartial parties. Must respect you for you.

East Alcove   The social doughnut hole of the lunchroom. See *West Alcove.*

enterdrained   A state of prolonged unconsciousness brought on by severely underwhelming entertainment; i.e., the yearly "Welcome Back, Wallingford Students" address. SYN: Comatastic.

exqueez-ay moi   *(French pronunciation.)* Excuse me.

fabulouz   *(French pronunciation.)* Fabulous.

Facebook limbo   The time and space between accepting and rejecting (or being accepted as or rejected as) a Facebook Friend. Either by mistake, see *backblogged,* or on purpose, see *Stalkbooking.*

the Hairy Eyeball   The double axel, triple salchow of all facial expressions: skill, practice, and flawless execution required to avoid fatalities.

hairy nip fit   A psychological condition of extreme upsetness—the common conniption fit (*nip fit*), only hairier. (Entirely unrelated to *the Hairy Eyeball*.)

Hawaiian Trops   The state of maximum tanness.

hello   **1.** Phone greeting. *Hello!?* **2.** Unbelievableness. *Hello!?* **3.** Can anyone hear me. *Hello!?* **4.** Excuse me, I was talking. *Hello!?* **5.** You are so unbelievably right. *Hello!?*

Hollywood Hair Bumpit   Hair enlargement device. Twice the volume of regular Bumpit.

Hyphenators   Those for whom one last name simply does not communicate it all; as in *Cosima Adrianzen-Fonseca* and *Emily Crawford-Green.*

insultosurus   from Latin, *insultinos* insulting + Greek, *-osaurus* person.

"I yove you" *"I love you"* while wearing super glossy lipstick.

La Coppa Coffee The center of the universe.

ledge *Legend* without that pesky second syllable.

Lylas Love You Like a Sister. Also: *L.Y.L.A.S.* SYN: Lyla.

moi *(French pronunciation.)* Me.

noblesse oblige The moral obligation of those of a higher standing, powerful auditorium seating, more adept use of ceramic flat iron, etc., to act with honor, kindness, generosity, etc., etc.

noof **1.** New person. **2.** The painful state of newness. **3.** The transferred student. **4.** The worst thing a person can be.

Obsessive Repulsive Disorder (ORD)   Mental disorder characterized by recurrent hair flips, laughter, and more hair flips all while totally pretending not to be doing it on purpose.

OMG   Last year's *OMG*.

OMGasp   This year's *OMG*.

populadder   The unseen hierarchical system of popularity, the bottom two-thirds of which don't count. Awareness of its existence is the key to being on it.

populartunity   A singular appropriate or favorable time or occasion as for populadder advancement. May never come again.

prepsicle   **1.** Head to toe prepsterness. **2.** Cute-preppy. **3.** The real deal. ANT: *Polo-poser, Abercrombie Zombie.*

Preptobismol   Taking the pink clothing thing way too far.

SABS   See and Be Seen. See *West Alcove.*

schnuggly   **1.** An item of clothing so cozy and old it must be banned from public use. **2.** Things that are so cute they make you nauseated.

sitch   *(British pronunciation.)* Situation.

Stalkbooking   When a person spends an unhealthy amount of time stalking another person's Facebook profile instead of actually getting a life.

tanorexia   *Tanorexia Nervoso.* A mental disorder such that the person thinks that no matter how tan they are, they're never tan enough; often acquired during or immediately following vacation breaks.

the Terminator   Living tissue over a metal endoskeleton sent back from the future to destroy the world, aka Ms. Hotchkiss.

totally   An agreement reached by all; *e.g., You: Tribb is distressingly fit. Us: Totally.*

Twittervention An orchestrated confrontation at La Coppa Coffee (without lattes or cranberry scones) to forcibly disarm Twitter account and get person to admit they need professional help or, at the very least, a fresh mani-pedi.

underpopular Not-popular through no fault of one's own; suffering from unpopularness. See *noblesse oblige.*

vous *(French pronunciation.)* You.

Wally **1.** A Wallingford Academy student. **2.** SLANG. A non-Aristobrat.

way An exclamation of moreness. Can be preceded by *so*, an exclamation of more more-ness; *e.g., Wally 1: Those new jeans are way great. Wally 2: So way great.*

West Alcove　The *only* place to eat your lunch. See *East Alcove.*

whinge-binge　**1.** Excessive indulgence in complaining; often revolving around "nothing to wear." **2.** An acceptable form of exercise.

Acknowledgments

To Jennifer Joel, Daniel Ehrenhaft, Niki Castle, Dominique Raccah, Kelly Barrales-Saylor, Kay Mitchell, Paul Samuelson, Kristin Zelazko, Danielle Trejo, Dawn Pope, Mallory Kaster, and Sarah Cardillo for their tireless faith, work, and support. To Tommy Jacoby, who makes my magic happen, and to Griffin Musser and Tallulah Musser, who inspire me every day. To Nan, Don, and Jordan Solow, whose palpable love of each other and of me has made me who I am. To my life-long friends, Karen Goldberg, Sharon Reidbord, and Juditta Musette. And to my newer lifelong friends, John Scott, Iole Taddei, and Nona and Randy Daron. To my board of advisors, Zoe Goldberg, Damon Jacoby, Ethan Jacoby, and Allen Meyer. To Winchester-Thurston, where this story was born, to Mill Valley Middle School, where the blanks were filled in, and to Shadyside Academy, who provided the boys when there were none.

About the Author

Jennifer Solow once attended an exclusive private school where her spot on the populadder wavered depending on whatever haircut she had at the time (long: good, short: not so good) and where the idea for this book began. Soon after, Jennifer moved to Manhattan, where she was an advertising creative director, wore a lot of cool clothes, and worked with a few famous guys named Spike. She now lives in Mill Valley with her husband and two children, where she is working on the next Aristobrats.

Visit her at www.jennifersolow.com, and find out more about the Aristobrats at www.thearistobrats.com.